a pinch of SALT

A Pinch of Salt

Published August 2017

ISBN—978-1548356217

Cover Design by:
Makeready Designs

Editing by:
Red Road Editing / Kristina Circelli

Proofreading by:
KMS Freelance Editing

Interior Design & Formatting by:
Christine Borgford, Type A Formatting

also by
BETHANY LOPEZ

Young Adult:
Stories about Melissa—series
Ta Ta for Now!
xoxoxo
Ciao
TTYL
With Love
Adios
Nissa: a contemporary fairy tale

New Adult:
Friends & Lovers Trilogy
Make it Last
I Choose You
Trust in Me
Indelible

Contemporary Romance:
A Time for Love Series
What Happened in Vegas (Prequel)
8 Weeks
21 Days
42 Hours
15 Minutes
10 Years
3 Seconds
7 Months

The Lewis Cousins Series

Too Tempting

Too Complicated

Three Sisters Catering

A Pinch of Salt

Romantic Comedy / Suspense:

Cupcakes Series

Always Room for Cupcakes

Cupcake Overload

Lei'd with Cupcakes

Women's Fiction:

More than Exist

Short Stories:

Christmas Come Early

Leap of Faith

Harem Night

Beau & the Beastess

Cookbook:

Love & Recipes

Love & Cupcakes

Children's:

Katie and the North Star

a pinch of SALT

a *three sisters catering* novel

BETHANY LOPEZ

Bethany Lopez

To the amazing Bloggers who are willing to take chances on writers they've never read before. Thank You for your support!

"To Three Sisters Catering," my sister Tasha said, her face beaming as she raised her glass of champagne. "May it be a smashing success."

"And make us happy," my twin, Dru, added as our glasses came together with a *tink*.

"And, allow us to share our gifts with others," I said, my eyes tearing up as I looked at the happy faces of my two favorite people in the world.

"*Salude*," we chimed, then tipped the pretty flutes back.

I sighed as the chilled bubbly liquid trailed down my throat. Champagne tasted happy, like a celebration, and drinking it I just *knew* we'd made the right choice in opening our own business. Even if our Aunt Priscilla told us we were nuts, or the guy who ran the restaurant on the corner glared at us every time we walked by . . . I felt it in my gut.

I'd always dreamed of not only cooking and baking for a living, but also of doing it my own way, in my own business. It just so happened that my sisters were my best friends who just so happened to share the same dream of being their own bosses.

"Momma would be so proud," Tasha said, her smile dimming a bit at the memory of our mother.

"She'd have said, '*forget the champagne, this calls for tequila,*'" Dru added softly, causing Tasha and me to laugh.

Rather than respond, I raised my glass in memory of our mother, and took a sip.

We'd taken the death of our mother very hard. She'd always been our rock, our sounding board, and our champion. We'd talked to various doctors and specialists, but in the end, the best we could do was be there, and make her comfortable.

This is for you, Momma. I swear, I'll do everything in my power to make this business work, and I'll take care of my sisters just like you'd want me to.

The chimes in the window made a beautiful melody, even though the windows were closed, and I knew it was our mother acknowledging my promise.

"I can't believe we get to move into our new building tomorrow and *actually* get started," Dru said excitedly. After months of planning and paperwork, it was hard to believe that our dream was finally coming to fruition.

"We're going to be crazy busy for the next few months, so I say we enjoy a nice dinner, then get some rest," I said practically, my mind already plotting out all the things I wanted to do in the kitchen.

"That sounds good, Millie, but first, we need to make a little pit stop."

"What for?" Dru asked Tasha.

"Tequila, of course," our raven-haired sister replied, and I went from daydreaming about stocking my new pantry to hoping I didn't wake up on my first day as a business owner with a massive hangover.

Millie

"Where the hell is Dru?" Tasha asked with a scowl as she stomped into my kitchen.

"Ah, I think she said she was going to check out decorations for the upcoming Wilson event," I answered as I rolled out dough on the floured table. "Why, what's up?"

"Mrs. Chapman just corned me for forty-five minutes about her daughter's baby shower," Tasha complained. "Dru promised me she'd handle it. She knows how that woman drives me batty."

"Where'd she catch you?" I asked as I kneaded.

"On my way out of the bathroom at the deli."

"Yikes," I said with a chuckle.

"She blocked the sink, so I had to listen to her gripe while I waited to wash my hands. She held me hostage, Mills."

I laughed at the look of pure horror on my younger sister's face.

"What else do you have this afternoon?" I asked, trying to take her mind off of her hostage situation.

"I'm going to stop by the printers and pick up the new business cards, then run over to the event space and make sure everything is on schedule for tonight. Can you hold down the fort?"

"Sure thing," I replied, smacking my lips together to blow her a kiss, since my hands were covered in dough.

"Thanks, babe," Tasha said, then left as quickly as she'd entered.

Three Sister's Catering had started out as strictly a catering business, but over the last year we'd added a small seating area and counter in the front of the store. Now, not only did we offer a full catering menu for events, but we sold assorted coffee, tea, and pastries.

We'd never planned on having a storefront, it had just happened organically.

I loved trying out new recipes and baking when I didn't have an order for catering, and I'd ended up with an abundance of product. Initially, I'd just bring some out when Tasha or Dru were meeting with clients, then it had morphed into a daily occurrence.

Now, we were open every morning, except Mondays, for people to stop in and grab a snack.

Dru had relished the opportunity to decorate the front of the house, and had made the little dining area into a warm and sophisticated place to stop and enjoy a quick break.

I was just putting the bread in the oven for tonight's bridal shower, when I heard the telltale jingle of the door being opened in the front.

"Be right out," I called as I gave my hands a good scrub and took off my dusty apron.

"Okay," a male voice returned.

I checked the small mirror I'd secured on the walk-in, to make sure I didn't have flour on my face, then walked out front with a smile for the waiting customer.

I stumbled a little at the sight of him.

Tall and thin, but with a nice set of biceps peeking out of his shirt, so you knew he was fit. A mop of wavy brown hair, a sweet, if somewhat panicked-looking face, and, *be still my heart*, glasses.

"Good morning," I managed, my tone coming out somewhat breathless as I tried to maintain a warm but professional demeanor.

"It will be, if you can help me," he replied hopefully, wringing his hands together as his eyes took on a doe-like quality.

Yes, I thought, *I can help you with whatever you need, just look at me like that every day for the rest of my life.*

"What can I do for you?" I asked, sure my cheeks were turning red.

Then he smiled, and two dimples appeared.

Seriously? I looked around the store for hidden cameras. *Are my sisters playing tricks on me? This guy cannot be real. Or any more adorable.*

"I know it's last minute, but I have an emergency. I need to hire you to cater my daughter's ninth birthday party."

And, there it is . . . the punchline. Mr. Adorable Dimples is married with a family.

I looked down at his ringed finger, smothered my disappointment, and gave him an apologetic smile.

"I'm sorry, we don't do children's parties."

When his face fell, I wanted to snatch the words back.

"We just don't have those types of decorations on hand," I added, hoping to soften the rejection. "There's a party supply store around the block; I'm sure they'll have what you need."

He shook his head and I tilted my head back to get a better look at him. *Damn, he was really tall.*

"I wish it were that simple. Kayla's outgrown the kind of birthday party I could give her. If we were still talking about *Frozen*, I could turn our living room into a winter wonderland and decorate the shit out of it." He winced and said, "Sorry," and I assumed he was talking about swearing. *Which, jeez, could he get any cuter.*

"What does she want?" I asked, even though I knew I should send him on his way and get back to work. I found I didn't want him to leave yet.

I was such a brat.

"A *tea party,*" he replied, making tea party sound like a bad word. "I've never even had a *drop of tea*, let alone made an entire party out of it."

I bit back a chuckle at his obvious distress, and asked, "Can't your wife help?"

His face looked pained, then he let out a sigh and said, "She, uh, left us, almost a year ago. We haven't heard from her since, so . . . no, I'm on my own with this one."

"I'm so sorry," I managed, feeling like a giant heel for getting so personal. I took a step forward, intent on touching his arm to offer comfort, then stopped when I realized what I was doing.

He waved off my apology and ranted, "Kayla's best friend had a tea party for her birthday, and all K could talk about was the little sandwiches and the pretty cups." He looked at me with wide eyes. "I know how to make two-fisted sandwiches, but finger sandwiches . . ."

He ran a hand through his hair, which was longer on top and short on the sides, and I bit my lip so I wouldn't smile at his adorable frustration.

"When does Kayla want this tea party?" I asked, even though I knew we didn't have time in our schedule to fit in a last-minute event.

"Saturday."

My mind started working as I thought about everything I had

to do in the next two days, and what we had on hand to make a little girl's ninth birthday tea party magical.

I walked around the counter and picked up our book, then flipped through the pages until I got to the event sheets.

"Here," I said, walking back to him with a clipboard and pen. "Fill this out with the date, time, place, and budget, and I'll see what I can do."

"Seriously?" he asked, his handsome face blossoming with hope.

"Seriously," I replied with a nod, then gasped when he crushed me to him in a bear hug.

"You're a lifesaver," he said, but all I could focus on were his long arms around my body, and my cheek plastered against his warm chest. It was deliciously firm, he smelled *amazing*, and I could hear the soothing sound of his beating heart. "An *angel*," he amended, then let me go.

I looked up at his smiling face, and my heart rolled over like a happy little gymnast.

Oh, boy . . .

He filled out the sheet and handed it to me with a sweet grin.

"I'll talk with my sisters and be in touch," I said as I looked down at the paper, then back up at him. "Jackson."

"I can't wait, Millie," Jackson replied, then winked at me, *winked at me*, and walked out the door.

I stood there for a moment, frozen in place by that wink, wondering how he knew my name. Then I remembered . . . it was sewn into my chef coat.

Jackson

Hugging her had probably been a bad idea, but, *damn*, it sure felt good.

It started out innocently enough. I really had stepped into Three Sisters Catering with the intention of begging, pleading, and bartering for a party for Kayla. Then she'd stepped out from the back . . . the sexiest brunette in a chef's coat I'd ever seen.

And the way her curves had fit snuggly against me, her head resting perfectly just below my chin . . . Well, let's just say my body hadn't reacted to a woman in that way since well before my wife left me.

I'd ended up stuttering and stumbling my way out of there. I think I *winked* for God's sake.

What a tool.

The important thing was that she'd said yes, they'd consider catering K's party. I'd been trying so hard to give Kayla everything she needed since Julie had walked out of our lives. I couldn't always give her what she wanted monetarily, but she knew she was the most important thing in my life, and I really wanted to make this birthday special. It was the first one since her mother disappeared, and I needed to prove that we could do this without her, that *I* could do this without her.

With the help of a catering company, that is.

"Running behind, Jackson?" Principal Wiggins called as I rushed through the entry door of the high school where I worked.

"Yeah, sorry," I called with a wave as I headed toward my classroom, pulling open the door just as the final bell rung.

"Busted," one of the students called out as I walked to my desk with a sheepish smile.

"Tardy, Mr. H," another student said.

"Yeah, yeah," I said with a chuckle. "Calm down."

Since my class was an Advanced English class, most of the students I had were there because they wanted to be, not just to fill a mandatory block on their schedule. We'd been in school for a couple months now, so I knew most of my students pretty well, and they knew what kind of teacher I was. I'd never been late before, so they had to give me shit, even though I was usually understanding when one of them were tardy.

"Car break down?"

"Alarm didn't go off?"

"Dog ate your homework?"

I let them get it all out while I placed my things on my desk and got out my lesson plan. Once I walked to the center of the room, they knew I was ready for business, and the good-natured taunts died down.

"*Hamlet*," I began, adjusting my glasses slightly as I surveyed the faces in the room. "Act three, scene one. Let's discuss."

It was one of those days where I was already exhausted by lunch. I was distracted, thoughts of Kayla's birthday and the morning's discussion of *Hamlet* buzzing around in my brain, so I didn't realize that I was about to run into one of the other teachers until I was right up on her.

"Oh," Rebecca Webber cried, as I reached a hand out to steady her.

"Sorry," I said as I took a step back.

I caught the slight blush on the history teacher's cheeks as she replied, "That's okay."

I nodded, then walked around her into the lounge. I headed to the table, where I sat with the other two male teachers in my school. Rob, who taught Algebra One, and Tyson, who taught Health and Physical Education.

They were already there, catching up on their weekend, when I sat down and started pulling out the items from my homemade lunch, which was identical to the one I'd made for my daughter that morning.

"'Sup, Jackson?" Rob asked as he downed the soda that he'd sworn to his wife he'd give up.

"I was late today," I admitted as I opened the baggie that held my peanut butter and Nutella sandwich. "You should have seen the look on Wiggins' face. It's not like I make a habit out of it or anything."

"I wouldn't worry about it," Ty said with a wave of his hand. "Sounds like he's pissed off about shit at home, at least that's the word on the streets. It's not personal; he knows you're one of the best around."

"Why was Mr. Perfect late anyway?" Rob asked with a grin, so I knew he was just messing with me.

"I stopped off at that catering business on Main, the one across from Prime Beef."

"That place is hot," Ty said. "I always book a table if I have a lady

I want to impress. I'm talking about Prime Beef, not the catering place. I've never been there."

"I have, they have those delicious breakfast pastries," Rob answered.

"Anyway, Kayla wants to have a tea party for her birthday, and since I haven't the first idea how to make that happen, I thought I'd give them a try."

"A *tea party*? What the hell do you do at one of those?" Rob asked.

"I don't know, eat tiny sandwiches and drink tea, I guess," I replied, then looked around to make sure no one was paying attention to our conversation before lowering my voice and adding, "The woman who works there is the hottest woman I've ever seen."

That sparked their interest, so they both leaned in closer.

"What does she look like?" Ty asked.

"'Bout five-four, five-five, with perfect curves, full lips, and the eyes of an angel."

"Hair?" Rob asked, causing Ty and me to give him matching looks. "What, you know I'm a hair man."

I shrugged. "It's dark and long, but hard to really tell because it was up in a bun. Which gave me unadorned access to her perfect face . . . She was nice, sweet even, and when I hugged her . . ."

"Hugged her?" Rob asked.

"Damn, Jackson, you work fast," Ty added with a chuckle.

"It was an impulse; I didn't mean to attack her or anything. She said she'd see what they could do to help me with the party, and I automatically hugged her."

"And it was?"

"Perfect," I admitted. "She smelled sweet, felt even better, and tucked right in and hugged me back."

"Wow," Ty said, and I knew he and Rob were thinking the

same thing I was. This was the first time I'd had even an ounce of attraction for a woman since Julie left.

"Are you going to ask her out?" Rob asked.

"I don't know," I admitted. It was complicated, what with me being a single dad who was technically still married. But, I'd left that store feeling something I hadn't felt in a really long time: *excited*.

I looked my friends in the eye as I opened my tapioca pudding and said, "You know what? I think I will."

Millie

"What's this?" Dru asked, the tone of her voice causing me to look up from tarts I was finishing up for tonight's event.

It took me a minute to realize what she was talking about, as she waved a piece of paper in the air.

"Oh, it's a last-minute tea party for a little girl," I replied, trying to sound like it was no big deal.

"No shit, last minute," my twin exclaimed, one hand on her hip, while she used the other to shake the paper at me. "I don't have time for this. *Literally*, don't have time. Why did you say we'd take this on, Millie? You know we're jam-packed for the next four days."

"I know that, I do, and I don't expect you to do a thing. I'll take care of it."

"You'll take care of it."

"Yup," I said, then grew wary when Dru narrowed her eyes at me. My sister never missed a thing.

"*Why, Millie?*" she asked as she stalked toward me. "Why, after a year of cooking and baking, *like the genius you are*, but not crossing over into event planning, management, or budgeting, will you be taking over this event on your own?"

Shit, I need to get her off the scent . . .

"Because," I began as my mind raced. Although I was the oldest by two minutes, my twin always seemed to know what I was going to do before I did, and I didn't want her to read anything into this tea party. I was only trying to help out a father and his daughter who'd had a rough time. *That was it . . . no hidden agenda here.* "I know how busy we are, and I also know that when I'm done with the food, you and Tash will still be busy pulling off another successful event. So . . . when the man came in needing help with his daughter's birthday, and I could see how desperate he was, I figured it wouldn't kill me to step out of the kitchen and pull off this small event."

Dru was watching me closely, so I continued my verbal vomit.

"Plus, this may gain us new clients *and* give us a chance to branch out in a new direction. I can handle it, Dru, promise."

"But, we'd decided months ago that we weren't going to do children's parties."

"True," I said with a nod, wishing I'd hear the sound of a customer entering the building so I could get out of this situation. "But, it's a tea party, which we've done in the past. So, although it's *technically* for a child, it's not *exactly* a children's party, at least not in the sense that we'd spoken about. No piñatas, or cartoon characters . . . *and*, we have supplies in the back already, so, really, it was a no-brainer."

"A no-brainer, huh?"

"Yup."

"And, did this *Jackson* have anything to do with your sudden interest in *stepping out of the kitchen*?" Dru asked as she looked down at the event sheet, then back up at me.

I felt the blush rise up from my neck, and watched Dru's lips turn up as she grinned victoriously.

Busted.

"Tell me," she demanded, so I did.

"Oh my Gosh, Dru, you wouldn't believe it. At first, I thought you and Tash had sent him in here to trick me or something," I admitted, grabbing a towel to wipe my hands as I crossed to her. "Tall, *crazy tall*, with a runner's body and brown hair that's short on the sides, but kind of floppy on top. And he had dimples, *and glasses* . . . It was like he walked out of the pages of my sixteen-year-old self's diary."

"Wow," Dru replied, then took in my face and asked, "So, what's the catch?"

"Married," I admitted with a frown. "I mean, he said his wife walked out and left him and their daughter, Kayla, a year ago, but, he was still wearing the ring."

"Ouch, that's terrible. For them, I mean, and for you. I'm sorry the man of your dreams walks in and he's already taken, but, if it's been a year, it must be really over, right? Maybe he just forgot to take it off."

I knew Dru was trying to see the bright side of things, and wanted me to be happy, but I wasn't sure that I should go there.

"I don't know," I replied. "It seems like a pretty complicated situation. I'm just going to do my best to give that little girl the best tea party she's ever seen. She deserves it. I can't even fathom our mom ever willingly leaving us."

"That's cause it wouldn't happen," Dru said with a sad smile. "But, you're right, it should be about the girl. I'll take you in the back and show you what we have on hand for a tea party. You should be set, all you'll need to do is make the food, set up, and clean up, and it should go off without a hitch."

"Thanks, Dru. I know it puts us in a tight spot, but I wouldn't have agreed to it if I didn't believe I could pull it off."

"I know," my sister said with a smile as she threw an arm around my shoulder. "You're such a softy."

"Am not," I argued, even though I knew I totally was.

"Yeah, right. I've known you for almost all of your twenty-eight years, so I consider myself an expert of the subject. This Jackson guy was lucky that it was you he ran into and not me or Tash. Maybe it was fate," Dru suggested with a nudge of her shoulder.

"Stop."

"What? Mom always said she'd make sure we'd find our perfect partners, even if she had to meddle from the other side. Maybe she sent Jackson your way."

"You're ridiculous," I said, shoving her softly as we walked into the back room.

Dru just laughed, but her words played over and over again in my head. And, despite my rational brain telling me that getting involved with Jackson would be an unwise decision, my heart welled with something that felt a lot like hope.

Jackson

"You want a snack, K?" I asked as my daughter settled at the kitchen table to do her homework.

We had a strict *do your homework first thing after school* policy, so our evenings were usually the same. Kayla would walk the two blocks from her school to mine, we'd ride home together, and she'd do her homework while I made dinner. After, she usually caught up with one of her friends while I graded papers or worked on lesson plans, and before bed, we'd watch a couple episodes of whatever show we were binge-watching.

Currently, we were on *The Goldbergs*, which we both found hilarious.

"Sure," Kayla replied with a half shrug as she started on her math worksheet.

I smiled at the back of her head, thinking how great it was that we were finally in a place where we were both content, and my daughter was happy.

Julie's abandonment had hit us both hard, and Kayla had taken quite a while to recover. I'd spent many nights holding her while she cried herself to sleep. It was hard for me, a thirty-year-old man, to understand why my wife of nine years had left without looking back. It was *impossible* for our eight-year-old daughter to comprehend.

She went from having her mom drive her to gymnastics, help her with her homework, and laugh with her over *Girl Meets World*, to listening to her mother tell her she needed a life of her own, then walk out the door.

I swear, if I ever saw Julie again, I'd kill her for those words alone.

My wife and I had never been over the moon in love with each other, but we'd shared a healthy relationship, love for our daughter, and what I'd thought had been an unbreakable support for one another.

Her leaving had totally blindsided me.

I was placing a plate of cut-up apples and a spoonful of peanut butter on a plate in front of Kayla when my cell phone started to ring.

When I looked at the unknown number, my heart clenched like it always did when I wondered if this was the day Julie was going to reach out.

There's no way she would actually leave her daughter and never look back, right? I mean, me, I could get, but Kayla? I'd never understand it.

"Uh, *hello*," I managed, becoming embarrassed at the nerves in my tone. I saw Kayla glance up from her sheet, and my heart sank at the look of hope on her face.

"Hello, is this Jackson?" a light, sweet voice asked, and I let out a sigh of relief.

It was Millie, from the catering place.

"It is," I replied, unable to keep the smile off of my face.

"Hey, this is Millie, from Three Sisters Catering."

"It's great to hear from you, Millie," I replied, and dammit, it really was. I hadn't been this excited to talk to a girl on the phone since high school.

I could tell she didn't know how to respond, because I heard a nervous laugh, then she said, "I'm, ah, calling to let you know that we're all set for Saturday. I'll plan to arrive at two to set up and be ready to serve from three to four. Are there any allergies or dislikes I need to know about?"

"Um, no, I don't think so," I replied, then added, "Thank you so much. I know it was last minute, and not something you would normally even do. You're really saving me here. I can't thank you enough."

"It's no problem," Millie replied, before pausing and saying, "I'll contact you if I have any questions, but I think you covered it all on the sheet. I'll see you Saturday."

"I can't wait," I said, truthfully.

"Goodbye, Jackson."

"Goodbye. And, thanks again."

I pressed the end button, still smiling, then glanced up to see Kayla watching me with an odd expression.

"Who was that?" she asked, her tone surprisingly surly.

"*That* was your good news," I replied, ignoring her tone and crossing to lean over the table, stopping when my face was inches from hers. "You're not going to believe it."

"What?" Kayla asked, her tone still wary, but her face starting to react to my excitement.

"*That* was the catering company that's going to be here to put on the best tea party ever, for my favorite daughter's birthday."

"Really?" she squealed, all surliness gone.

"Really, really."

Kayla jumped up and rounded the table to jump into my waiting arms.

"Thanks, Daddy," she murmured, and my heart filled with joy.

"Anything for my baby girl," I replied, bending slightly to drop a kiss on the top of her head.

Kayla pulled back and grinned up at me.

"I can't wait to tell everyone. A sleepover *and* a tea party? This is going to be the *best birthday ever*!"

I chuckled as she practically danced back to her seat.

"Can I call them?" she asked, her eyes wide and hopeful.

I just smiled and gave my head a small shake.

"After homework."

"Boo," Kayla replied, but she was still beaming.

I went back to my dinner prep, my heart light as I watched my daughter go back to her homework with a smile on her face, and I sent a silent thanks to Millie, the sweet and sexy chef who'd unwittingly saved the day.

Millie

I may have gone a little overboard, but once I'd started thinking about different tea party ideas, I couldn't help but want to make it a birthday this little girl would never forget.

I'd chosen a delicate tea set with pretty pink rosebuds, lots of pretty pastel decorations, and flowers. Tons of flowers.

Colorful macaroons, sweet little sandwiches, and tiers of cupcakes, coupled with strawberry punch, lots of fun candies, and cut outs for a photo booth, all teamed together to make a nine-year old's birthday dream a reality.

My sisters and I had loved playing dress up as girls, and being in the kitchen had always been my passion, so it hadn't been hard to tap into my inner child when deciding what to do for Kayla.

I just hope she likes it.

I was getting out of my 4Runner and heading to open the back when the front door opened and Jackson came out of the house and jogged toward me.

I don't know why, but I found him jogging toward me in loose jeans and bare feet strangely sexy.

"Hey, hi, how are you?" Jackson asked as he approached, causing me to smile up at him.

"Great, how are you?" I countered as I opened the back and bent to pull out a container.

"Let me help," he said, suddenly right behind me. His breath hit my neck and I barely suppressed a shudder. "I'm great as well. So excited that you're here . . . er . . . that you could do this party for K."

"I'm happy we could fit it in. I had a lot of fun putting it together," I admitted. "I hope she loves it."

He grabbed a couple containers out of the back and gave me a sincere grin.

"I'm sure she will."

I let him lead the way into the sweet little ranch-style house. It had an open floorplan, with the large living room leading into the kitchen and eat-in dining area. The style was comfortable, but contemporary. It definitely had a woman's touch.

"You can use anything you'd like. I figured we'd set up the table for the tea party, but that's about as far as I got."

"Don't worry, I brought everything," I assured him, then went back out for another load, with Jackson hot on my heels.

"So, how have you been?" Jackson asked, and I could swear he sounded as nervous as I felt.

"Great. Busy. We have a total of five events this weekend, including yours, so I spent most of my night, and morning, in the kitchen."

"Wow," he said, catching my eyes with his as he lifted the box full of china. "I hope I didn't make things more difficult. Sorry about the last-minute request."

"Careful," I warned, then gave him a warm smile. "It's no problem, really. I usually stay in the kitchen, chained to the stove," I chuckled softly. "My twin sister, Dru, she's the event planner and decorating queen, while our younger sister, Tasha, is the brains behind the business. She's our business manager and accountant. They are really the faces of the company. Scheduling, planning, and executing events. I'm much happier planning the menus and making the food. This is actually the first event that I've headed up myself."

"Well, thanks, really. I'm sorry to give you more work, but I'm extremely grateful that you agreed to help."

Jackson's smile was so sincere that I felt my heart swell as my stomach did a nervous little dance.

"It's my pleasure," I replied, feeling my cheeks warm as I took out the last few bags and shut the door. "Those must be getting heavy," I added, indicating the china and hoping to get the attention off of myself and get to work. I hated being the center of attention, and appreciated the fact that my sisters were happy to take the spotlight off of me and allow me to hide in my kitchen.

We got everything inside and put on the counter, then Jackson said he was going to go check on Kayla, and I got started.

First, I laid out a pastel-pink table cloth and covered it with a white lace runner, then I set up my serving platters and display racks. I covered the chairs with matching pink covers, then tied a large white bow to the back of each.

When Jackson walked back into the room, I was strategically placing the vases of flowers that I'd pre-arranged around his dining area.

"How long was I gone?" Jackson asked, his head swiveling around comically.

I laughed and said, "I'm used to working fast."

"Do you need any help?" he asked, pushing his glasses up the bridge of his nose.

"Yeah, could you take all of the candy necklaces out of the

wrapping and hang them on that jewelry holder?"

While Jackson began opening the plastic bags, I crossed to my bakery boxes and began organizing the goodies on the table.

"So, Millie," Jackson began, causing me to look up from my macaroon placement. "I was wondering if you're . . . *taken*, and if not, do you think you might want to go out sometime . . . with me?"

I blinked slowly as the blood rushed through my body, but as I opened my mouth to speak a squeal came from the hallway.

"Oh. My. Goodness."

A pretty little girl, with long wavy hair and a huge smile, stood there with her hands up in the air. She was already dressed for her party in a pretty pink dress that matched my decorations perfectly.

I gave myself a mental high five, then watched as Jackson smiled beautifully at his daughter as he crossed the room and lifted her in his arms.

"Do you like it?" he asked, laughing as she threw her arms around his neck.

"I love it, Daddy!" she cried, and I felt the back of my eyes burn.

Jackson put her back on her feet and she ran over to where I was finishing up the table.

Kayla placed her hand on the lace and ran her hand over it reverently, then looked up at me with her father's smile and asked, "Did you do this?"

I nodded and replied, "Guilty," then gasped when the little girl crashed into me and hugged my waist.

Six

Jackson

The next couple hours were a whirlwind of giggles, tiny sandwiches, and enough sugar to ensure that I was in for a long night.

Millie was amazing.

Not only were her decorations on point, and her food delicious, she'd kept the girls entertained and had successfully given my little girl the party of her dreams. I hadn't seen Kayla smile this much since her mother left, and I was eternally grateful to Millie for that.

If I hadn't already planned on asking Millie out, and I guess I sort of had, even though we'd been interrupted, I definitely would have wanted to take her out after seeing her interact with my daughter and her five boisterous friends.

Now the tea party was over, and the girls had all escaped to the backyard to jump on the trampoline while Millie and I cleaned up.

She was currently boxing up the props she'd used for the tea party photo booth, while I was slyly popping leftover macaroons in my mouth.

"I saw that," Millie said with a chuckle.

I turned, mouth full and a sheepish look on my face, to see her holding the sunglasses prop over her eyes and waggling her eyebrows.

"Sorry," I mumbled, covering my mouth with my hand so I wouldn't show her my food. "I couldn't resist."

"Don't be sorry," she replied, dropping the glasses in the box. "I take it as a compliment."

Once I swallowed, I said, "And you should. Everything was amazing. Really, I can't thank you enough. K had a blast."

"I did too," Millie responded with a sweet smile. "I didn't realize how much fun I was missing out on by always being in the kitchen. I'll have to talk to Dru and Tasha about helping out more."

"You're a natural."

"Thanks," she said, her cheeks turning pink, and I could tell she was uncomfortable with praise. Millie pointed at the leftover food and changed the subject. "Do you have Tupperware containers you want that in, or do you want me to leave the boxes?"

"I have something, just a sec."

I rounded the island in my kitchen and crouched down to get to my containers, while mentally prepping myself to re-approach the question I'd asked earlier. I understood her not wanting to answer in front of the girls, but I was dying to know if she'd go out with me, and I was slightly terrified to ask again.

I'd barely worked up the courage to ask her out once, the thought of doing it again had my palms sweating.

"Here we are," I said as I popped up and placed the assorted rectangles on the counter.

"Perfect," Millie replied, crossing the room with the dishes of leftovers.

I cleared my throat as she started placing the items in the

containers, but when I raised my head to pose my question again, Millie beat me to it.

"About what you asked earlier," she began, her head bent as if she were laser focused on boxing up leftovers. "I just don't know if it's a good idea . . ."

My stomach dropped as disappointment filtered through me.

"Oh," I began, unsure how to respond.

"It's not that I don't want to go out with you," Millie said in a rush, her eyes coming up to find mine, so I could see the sincerity in her gaze. "I do. I mean, we only just met, but I like you, Jackson."

"Then why?" I asked, confused by her contradicting words.

The she glanced down at my left hand, and I dropped my head to see what she was looking at.

My wedding ring.

I wanted to slap myself in the head and apologize for being so obtuse. I honestly hadn't thought about the ring once over the last year, but how did I get Millie to believe I wasn't holding some torch for Julie?

"Have you ever worn a piece of jewelry for ten years and just sort of gotten used to it being there? Like I assume it is with earrings?" I asked, not really expecting her to answer, just hoping she'd understand. "I haven't lied to you."

"I know that," Millie replied quickly, her hand reaching out to cover mine. "I believe that you're separated, but I couldn't help notice that you still wear your ring. Plus, you share a beautiful daughter with the woman that you're *still* married to."

"Yes, it's complicated, but I promise you, it's over. I'm not waiting for her to come back and pick up where we left off. Hell, there's no way I'd take her back even if she wanted me to," I explained, hoping Millie could hear the sincerity in my voice.

Millie nodded, and as she worried her bottom lip between her teeth, I could tell she was still on the fence, which gave me hope. It meant she didn't *want* to say no.

"What if we just met for coffee?" I suggested. "We can take things slow . . . get to know each other."

I held my breath as I waited for her to reply. I could almost see the argument going on in her head, and I hoped that I came out on top.

Finally, Millie patted my hand before taking hers back, then smiled softly and said, "I'd like that."

Not even bothering to hold back, I grinned broadly and clapped my hands together once.

"*Fantastic.*"

I helped Millie load the decorations and tea set into her 4Runner, then walked her to the door and held it open as she got into the driver's seat.

"I'll call you to set up coffee," I said before shutting the door.

The desire to kiss her was great, but since I'd just promised to take it slow, I figured it was best to keep that desire in check.

"I look forward to it," Millie replied, then I shut the door and stood there as she drove away.

After she was out of sight, I looked down and twisted the gold band on my finger, then pulled it off and held it in the palm of my hand. It looked like it was time for me to pay more attention to the things I was holding on to, and start packing them away.

Also, it was time for me to find my wife.

Seven

Millie

"So, how'd it go with Mr. Adorable Dimples?" Tasha asked as we stretched out. We were off Mondays and that's when we got together with our adult recreation soccer league. The three of us had been playing soccer since we could walk, and enjoyed getting out and playing whenever we could.

Which wasn't as much as we'd like, now that business was booming.

"I already told Dru the whole story last night . . . It was good," I said vaguely, hiding my smirk when Tasha started to pout.

"Well, I was working last night so I missed the girl talk. You can't hold that against me, Mills, I was bringing home the bacon," Tasha complained as she crouched down.

"Fine," I said with mock exasperation," I'll give you the cliff notes."

Tasha kept her eyes on me as she waited expectantly. She'd recently cut off her long black hair that had matched mine and Dru's in length into a cute bob, and dyed it a bright red. It totally suited her.

"The party was great, fantastic even. I had a blast decorating, and the girls loved it. I took pictures to show you guys, and for the website," I began, but Tasha waved her hand, encouraging me to get to the good stuff. "Jackson asked me out," I said with a shrug, then teased her by saying, "But, I said no."

"Wha?" Tasha cried, standing and putting her hands on her hips. "Why'd you do that? I thought he was your diary dream man. At least, that's what Dru said."

I raised my eyebrow at my twin, who just stuck out her tongue at me and continued stretching her quads.

"He's also *married*, and still wears his wedding ring," I replied, then sighed and added, "But, he assured me that the marriage is very much over, the ring was just an oversight, and we're going to meet up for coffee this week. So, *not* a date, just coffee."

"A coffee date," Dru said with a grin.

"*Shut up*," I replied, but couldn't hold back my answering smile. "I don't know, you guys, he scares me."

"Why?" Tasha asked. "Because you've been so focused on the business, and before that, Mom, that you haven't met a man for coffee, let alone had one between your legs, since you and Dru were at USC?"

"That's not true," I argued, offended and a little embarrassed about how right my younger sister was. "There was Joshua . . ."

"Ewww," my sisters groaned in unison.

"You mean that creeper guy who kept taking you to Anime movies and trying to get you to give him a handy in the theater?" Dru asked. "You really want to count *that* guy?"

"No, I guess not," I said with a frown, then threw myself back onto the grass and added, "Gosh, you guys, it has been a long time. A really, *really* long time. Maybe jumping back into things with a Mr. Adorable Dimples, who's not only a single father, but hasn't even divorced his wife yet, is not a good place to start. Maybe I need to wade into the shallow end first."

"Fuck the shallow end," Dru said, and I knew she dropped the F bomb to rankle me. She knew I hated it when she talked like that, which was exactly why she did it. "I say jump right into the deep end, clothes and all. It's time you had a little fun, Mills, and you like this guy. Go for it."

"Yeah," Tasha agreed. "I'm with Dru. Enjoy your coffee, then take him back to your apartment and jump his bones."

I laughed at Tasha, but before I could reply, our coach yelled out, "Are you ladies going to gab all day, or are you going to get out here and play some football?"

"Sorry, Coach," we all called, then jogged out to meet up with our team.

I sat on the bench for the beginning of the first half, my eyes on the field as my mind wandered to thoughts of Jackson. Almost as if I'd conjured him, I heard my phone signal a text, then discreetly pulled it out of the bag at my feet, my stomach dropping when I saw it was him.

Hey, Millie, it's Jackson. I was wondering if you'd rather meet during lunch, or after work, for coffee? I know you work early, but I wasn't sure when you took breaks, if you even take them. I can break away during lunch, or meet you after school. Whatever works for you. Sorry, I'm rambling . . .

After school? I'm pretty flexible. I can work my schedule around whatever date/time you'd like to meet.

Yes, I'm a teacher, did I not tell you that? I teach English at the high school. After school would be best, that way we won't be rushed. How does Wednesday at 3:30 sound?

Oh, that's wonderful. What a fun job. Wed at 3:30 works for me. Where do you want to meet?

Well, I can pick you up, if you'd like, then we can go to Rooster's, if that works?

Rooster's was a coffee shop on Main Street, just a couple blocks from our business.

"Hey, Millie, are you going to pay attention to the team, or your phone?" my coach called out, causing me to flush and reply, "Sorry, Coach." It seemed like that was all I could say today.

That sounds great. Have to go. Bye.

I looked up at our coach sheepishly, then turned the phone off and put it back in my bag. My head came up just in time to see Tasha dribbling down the field, then make a successful pass to Dru, who kicked it right into the goal.

"YEAH!" I yelled, jumping to my feet to cheer on my team.

"Millie, go in for Tampa," Coach said, and all thoughts of Jackson and coffee left me as I jogged out onto the field to join my sisters.

We had a game to win.

Jackson

I was finishing up my lesson plans for when we moved on to *Pride and Prejudice* next week, but my eyes kept drifting up to the clock. Much like my students, I couldn't wait for the bell to ring, signaling the end of the school day.

Normally, I stick around after school, grade some papers, straighten my room, and prepare for the next day, but today all I could think about was picking up Millie at three thirty.

I couldn't remember the last time I was this excited about anything. Sure, it was only coffee, but it didn't matter what we were doing, I couldn't wait to see her again.

The bell rang and I jumped up from my chair, pushing through my students as I tried to beat them out the door.

"Where's the fire, Mr. H?"

"Sorry . . . *Sorry*," I muttered as I reached the hallway, then started speed walking toward the exit closest to the teacher's parking lot.

"Jackson."

I bit off the curse before it passed my lips, then turned to see who was currently stalling my swift exit.

"Oh, hey, Rebecca. What's up?" I asked the history teacher, who was watching me nervously as she approached.

"Do you have a few minutes?" she asked, her voice timid, which was unusual.

"Actually, I'm on my way out," I said hastily, looking at my watch to emphasize the fact that I was in a hurry. "Can it wait until tomorrow?"

"Oh, yeah, sure," Rebecca replied, and I chose to ignore the disappointment on her face, because although we were always friendly with each other, whatever school-centric question she had couldn't be more important than going on the first non-date I'd had in over ten years.

"Thanks, Rebecca," I said, patting her arm distractedly before spinning on my heel and heading back for that door.

"Hey, Jacks," I heard called, and this time didn't hold my, *"Son of a bitch"* back, although I only whispered it under my breath.

I turned my head to see Ty jogging toward me.

"What's up, man?" I asked, not stopping, but rather keeping my pace while he fell in step beside me.

"So, you ready for your big date?" my friend asked, making me immediately regret telling him and Rob that I was meeting Millie today.

"Yup," I said as I pushed the door open.

"All right, brother, I just wanted to wish you luck, and tell you to be cool . . . Just be yourself."

"Thanks, Ty," I said, finally stopping when my feet hit the sidewalk. "I'm a little nervous, but more excited. Hopefully she'll see I'm sincere about everything with Julie, and this will be the beginning of something great."

"I hear that," Ty said, running a hand over his short dark hair before adding, "You deserve that, Jackson, after the shit Julie shoveled at you. But, hey, can I ask you a favor, for all of us here at school?"

"Yeah, man, what's that?" I asked, confused by his question.

"Can you let Rebecca down easy?"

"Rebecca?" I asked, looking over his shoulder to where Rebecca had just been standing.

"Yeah," he began, then sighed. "She's had a crush on you forever."

"What? No, she hasn't."

"Yeah, man, she has. You're the only one who hasn't noticed."

Shocked, I just looked at my friend, unable to respond.

"She's just been biding her time, waiting for you to be ready after the fiasco with Julie, and today, it looked like she was about to make her move. I know you're not interested, brother, I'm just asking that you go easy, yeah? You've got to see her every day. We all do."

I nodded absently, still trying to wrap my head around what I was hearing. Rebecca had always been nice enough, and we often helped each other out after school, sometimes chaperoning events together, but I'd never thought of her as anything more than a friend.

My stomach clenched at the thought of that awkward conversation.

"Of course, Ty, you know I wouldn't want to hurt her feelings."

"I know, Jacks, just wanted to give you a head's up."

"Thanks."

"I've got your back, you know that," Ty said with a grin, then clapped me on the back. "Have fun, and don't be afraid to be aggressive."

I chuckled at my friend, having no intention whatsoever in taking his advice, then *finally* made my way to the teacher's parking lot.

My watch told me I still had fifteen minutes to get to Three Sisters Catering, and although I'd wanted to be early, at least I'd still get there on time.

I'd pulled up in front of Millie's storefront with two minutes to spare. When I stepped out of my truck I saw Jericho Smythe standing outside of Prime Beef messing with his menu board.

"Hey, Jericho!" I yelled out, lifting my hand in a wave to my buddy, who owned the steakhouse. We were part of the same Fantasy Football league, and often got together with a group of guys to watch games. Plus, he served the best steak in town.

"How's it going?" Jericho asked in reply.

I shot him a thumbs up and a huge grin, then jogged around the truck so that I'd make it on time. I'd fill Jericho in later on why I didn't have time to catch up, being on time to pick up Millie was more important.

The door jangled as I opened it. The tables and chairs were empty, since they weren't currently serving, but it only took a moment before Millie stepped out from the back.

In a pale-blue dress with her hair hanging long and straight around her shoulders, she was the most beautiful woman I'd ever seen. I was momentarily stunned. Speechless.

I watched as Millie walked toward me, a small, uncertain smile playing on her lips, then I took a step toward her and reached out my hand. When she took it, I propelled myself closer and lowered my lips to her cheek, kissing her softly before saying, "You look gorgeous."

Millie

I was overcome by nerves. All morning I couldn't stop fretting over this coffee date with Jackson. I mean, what did I really know about the guy. Sure, I knew he was a good dad, his house was nice, and something about those glasses he wore made my body pulse, but I didn't really *know* him.

Shoot, I hadn't even known he was a teacher until he'd mentioned it in that text.

Although, out of all the professions out there, high school English teacher was better than assassin, or jewelry thief.

But, when I stepped out into the storefront and saw him standing there, not even trying to hide his pleasure at seeing me, I shoved my doubts to the side and decided to dive in.

It was just coffee, after all, it wasn't as if I was his new mail-order bride. There was no commitment being made.

"Thank you," I replied, when his compliment penetrated my thoughts. I'd probably tried on twenty different outfits before finally deciding on the blue dress. It was conservative, yet flirty. At least, that's what I hoped.

"Are you ready?" he asked, pushing his glasses up his nose in what I was beginning to realize was a nervous gesture.

"Yes," I replied, giving him a true smile. It was easier knowing that he was just as nervous as I was. "Let's go."

"It's a beautiful day, shall we walk?" Jackson asked, mockingly holding out his arm in a gallant gesture.

I laughed at his silliness and tucked my arm in his.

"I'd love that."

As we started on the short walk to the coffee house, I asked, "So, what made you get into high school English?"

"I always knew I wanted to be a teacher, and I've always loved literature, so it seemed like a no-brainer," Jackson replied easily. "I started out with your basic freshman English, but now I teach an advanced class, focusing on the classics, like Shakespeare, Austen, and Alcott, and it's great because the kids in my class choose to be there, so they actually want to learn what I'm teaching."

"Wow, that sounds wonderful," I replied, my heart pitter-pattering at the thought of Jackson laying down to read Jane Austen at night. "And very rewarding."

"It is," he agreed. Just then, the wind kicked up and his scent hit me. A bit of spice, with a hint of something I couldn't name. He smelled wonderful.

I was beginning to wonder what the hell was wrong with this guy. There had to be something. No one was this perfect.

Maybe he picks his nose or bites his toenails . . .

But as I looked at his profile, my hand warm on his arm, I hoped that I was wrong. I wanted him to be real.

"And for you," Jackson added, pulling me out of my thoughts. "It must be rewarding running your own business. A family business at that."

I nodded, then looked down at the ground as we walked and said, "After our mother died, we decided to do what she would have wanted us to, and follow our dreams. Sure, it was risky, but we learned the hard way that you need to go after what you want before it's too late."

"Hey," Jackson said, stopping on the sidewalk and putting his hand under my chin. As he was lifting it up to bring my eyes to his, I noticed that he was no longer wearing his wedding ring.

My heart leapt.

"I'm sorry about your mom," he said softly when our eyes met.

"Thank you."

"It takes a lot of bravery and strength to take a chance on doing what you love. I know your mother would be proud of you and your sisters."

All my worries and doubts fled at his words, and I knew I wanted to see where things went with him. I wanted this coffee date to be our beginning.

"I really appreciate that," I said with a small smile, then tugged on his arm to get us moving again. A half a block down, we came to the awning above Rooster's Coffee House, and I gave Jackson thanks when he held the door open for me to go inside.

The smell of coffee, pastries, and cinnamon assaulted me as I walked in, and turned to Jackson with a sigh.

"I love this place."

"I've never been," he admitted, "but it smells great."

Not only did it smell great, but it was decorated in a rustic, farmhouse style. Lots of distressed wood, tin fixtures, and, of course, roosters everywhere.

We walked to the counter, where he ordered a black coffee and croissant, and I ordered a salted caramel latte and a cranberry scone. Once we had our treats, we took the white iron bistro table in the back.

"Salted caramel, huh?" Jackson asked after he held out my seat, then took his own. "I've heard that's the current craze."

"You've never had anything salted caramel?" I asked, my jaw dropping slightly. "Candy, cupcakes, ice cream, latte, nothing?"

Jackson chuckled at my dramatic response and shook his head.

"Nope, the combo never appealed to me. I mean, salt on top of caramel, it just doesn't seem right."

"Sometimes a pinch of salt is all you need to take something bland, and make it absolutely delicious," I replied, holding my drink out to him. "Here, you have to try it."

Jackson accepted the challenge, taking my hot cup and lifting it to his lips. I was mesmerized by the sight of his lips on the rim of my cup, then laughed when he pulled away to reveal the slight whipped cream mustache that was left behind.

He darted his tongue out to wipe his lip clean, then his eyes darkened when he noticed I was watching, my breath stuck in my throat.

"Delicious," Jackson said gruffly, and I had to agree, *it was.*

Jackson

I was almost done with my coffee, and things had been going great, when Millie reached over and ran her finger over where my wedding ring used to be.

"I, ah, noticed that you took it off," she began, and I knew there was a question in there.

I closed my eyes for a moment, enjoying the light caress of her finger on mine, then opened them and gave her a wry smile.

"I'd known Julie all my life, our parents were friends, and we went to the same schools together," I said, turning my hand under hers and holding it in place. "We started dating in high school, which made our families happy, and we just sort of settled into things from there. It was never love at first sight, or a match made of passion." I paused, realizing my inner literature nerd was coming out, then I chuckled and continued, "Sure, we had the sweaty palms and stolen kisses of any teenaged relationship, but soon we just fell into an easy relationship. We went to college together, then Julie got pregnant and we moved back home to get married."

"Well, you got an amazing daughter out of it," Millie said, her hand squeezing mine compassionately.

"Yeah, K is the best thing that ever happened to me."

I realized we were both done with our drinks and snacks, but wasn't ready to leave yet, so I asked, "Would you like something else? A water?"

"Yeah, that would be great," Millie replied sweetly, and I felt relieved that she wasn't ready to end this thing yet either.

I excused myself to go to the counter and buy two waters from the barista, then looked back at Millie while I waited. She was sitting at our table, looking around the dining room with a smile on her lips. I hadn't really paid attention to my surroundings, but I followed her gaze and took in the décor of Rooster's.

It kind of reminded me of my grandparents' house . . . *Mental note, it's time to make a visit, Kayla and I haven't been to Grandma's in a few months.*

Once the mental note was cataloged in the calendar in my mind, I grabbed the waters and strode back to Millie.

"Where were we?" I asked as I placed her water on the table and took my seat.

"You moved back home to have Kayla," she supplied, then opened her water and said, "Thanks."

"You're welcome," I replied, then thought back to my time with Julie. "She dropped out of school and we got married, while I transferred here and started taking classes. We rented a crappy two-bedroom row house, but we were happy. Excited about the baby. A few years after I started teaching, we had enough money saved to put a down payment on the house I live in now. Our marriage was a partnership. We didn't fight, or have some deep-seated resentment about getting pregnant before marriage. We were just your normal family. When she said she was leaving, I was blindsided.

One hundred percent."

I lost my words as I thought back to that day, when Julie said she was leaving, and I swear, I thought she was joking. It had never occurred to me that we wouldn't spend our lives together.

"She said she needed to live her own life. That she'd given up everything to become a mother and wife, and she wanted to see what else was out there. I told her she was crazy, that she'd regret it, and asked how she could do that to Kayla . . ."

"What did she say?" Millie asked softly, her hand once again on mine.

I brought my eyes to Millie's, caught momentarily in the green and gold flecks I saw there.

"She said she was sorry, but that Kayla would grow to understand, and then she left." I sighed, then took a sip of my water. "I haven't heard from her since."

"What about your parents, or hers; are you all still close?"

"Yeah, my parents still live next door to hers, and Kayla spends time at both of their houses. She's the only grandchild for both, so they spoil her to death. We go to my parents every Sunday for brunch, so she sees them at least once a week, sometimes more."

"That's wonderful, that she gets to be close to her grandparents, and I'm sure it helps you a lot, that they're all so close."

I nodded as I thought about last Sunday, when we all celebrated Kayla's birthday together. She got to have her party with her friends, and then another with her family. She'd been over the moon, and even though I sometimes worried that we were all spoiling her too much, while we all tried to make up for her mother leaving, I couldn't regret making my little girl happy.

"I don't know how I would have made it without them," I admitted. "Whenever I have something going on at school, they help me out by watching her, and anytime she wants to go shopping, or get her nails done, my mom and Julie's, are always happy to take her."

"And, have they heard from Julie?" Millie asked gently. "Her parents?"

Shaking my head, I replied, "No, at least not that they ever told me, although I haven't asked in months. They felt just as abandoned as we did, and I know they've wondered where they went wrong. They were always very close, especially Julie and her dad, and he was just as baffled as I was when she left."

"That's terrible, I'm so sorry for you all," Millie said, then looked up at me through her eyelashes. "Do they also babysit when you go on dates?"

I fought back a grin at her question, knowing she was trying to find out if I'd been seeing anyone since Julie left. I liked that she wanted to know. I hoped that meant she wanted to see more of me, because I sure as hell wanted to see more of her.

"I don't know," I admitted. "I haven't dated anyone since Julie."

"Really?"

"Really," I replied, then I turned her hand in mine and brought her palm to my lips. I kissed her there once, a soft brush of the lips, then placed her hand back on the table. "But, I'm hoping that will change. Maybe they can babysit Friday night, while we go to Prime Beef?"

A beautiful smile blossomed over her face, and she gave a slight nod.

"I'd like that. Let me check our schedule and see what I can do."

"Do you have an event?"

"We always do. Our only day off is Monday, *but*, I can always take a break for dinner," Millie said, and although I was disappointed that I wouldn't get a full date with her, I loved the fact that she was willing to rearrange her schedule to fit me in. "It helps that Prime

Beef is right across the street," she added with a laugh.

"Okay, great. You check your schedule and see if you can swing it, and I'll check with my parents and see if they can take Kayla."

"Sounds like a plan," she said, and I fought back regret when she rose from her seat. "I'd better get back."

We walked back to Three Sisters hand in hand, Millie talking happily about the menu she'd prepared for a bridal shower they were catering that evening. All too soon, we were at her door and she was turning to me, her face flushed with pleasure, as she said goodbye.

"Thanks for going with me today," I said, reaching out to tuck a long lock of hair behind her ear, my heart racing when she turned her cheek toward my touch. "I had a great time, and can't wait until Friday."

Her face went soft at my words, and I noticed her eyes were trained on my lips.

Although it had been almost fifteen years since I experienced a first kiss with a woman, I knew the moment was right, so I took a step closer, one hand on her waist and the other cupping her cheek. Millie's eyes fluttered closed as I bent my head, and a soft moan escaped her lips when I brushed mine against hers.

She tasted of caramel and cream, and when I ran my tongue lightly across the seam of her lips, she opened for me, and I accepted her invitation.

The kiss was sweet, with just a hint of reckless, and I knew when she sagged slightly against my chest that it was time to pull away. With what felt like the strength of twenty men, I did just that, then dropped one more kiss on her lips before taking a step back.

I knew I'd keep a picture of that dreamy look on Millie's face with me forever, and when I walked to my truck, there was a spring in my step.

Eleven

Millie

I floated through the storefront, across the kitchen, and into the office in the back I shared with my sisters.

It was a good-size room. Big enough that you could fit three desks, some bookshelves, and a couple chairs. My desk was the smallest, since most of my work was done in the kitchen, with Tasha and Dru having full-size desks, which were always put to use.

While Dru's was completely covered, and cluttered at all times, Tasha's was organized and always clean. Dru had an old oak desk with decorating magazines, a large organizer, and swatches all over it, while Tasha's had a modern feel, with chrome finish and smooth lines.

My desk was shoved up against the corner with a small purple chair tucked under it. It was white and feminine, and held only my recipe cards, cookbooks, and notes full of ideas.

Tasha and Dru had been talking about the wedding reception we had this upcoming Saturday, but when I walked in their heads turned to me and their conversation stopped. Dru's lips turned up into a grin, and Tasha slapped her hand on the table, causing me to jump out of my daze.

"You didn't take him to your apartment," Tasha complained.

I chuckled softly. "You knew that wasn't going to happen."

"A girl can dream . . ."

"Something happened though," Dru said, still grinning. "I'm thinking the only thing that could put that dazzled look on Mills' face is a big, sloppy kiss."

"Ooooh," Tasha exclaimed, scooting forward on her chair and clapping her hands. "Do tell."

"You guys," I began, then sighed and spun in a circle, letting my dress flair up, much like I had after my first kiss in high school. "He's . . . *amazing*."

"She's smitten," Tasha said, then pushed back and spun her chair in a circle.

"I think you're right," Dru agreed, her eyes soft on me. "The girl's in deep smit."

Tasha chuckled and I shook my head.

"He teaches Shakespeare and Austen to teenagers . . . He talks about his daughter like she's a miracle, and he kisses like a dream," I gushed, then fell in the overstuffed floral chair that was in front of Tasha's desk with an exaggerated sigh. "I'm in trouble. I really, *really* like him, and I don't even know him yet."

"Why does Millie get all the luck? Perfect boobs, the ability to make people weep with her talent in the kitchen, and now? She's caught the eye of a swoony, dimple-having, glasses-wearing, romantic, who's great with kids." This Dru asked Tasha dramatically, before turning to me and saying, "We shared a womb, you know . . . you could have left *something* for me."

I rolled my eyes at my gorgeous, funny, and equally talented twin.

"Pulease," I replied sarcastically. "The one thing you've never lacked, my dear sister, is confidence."

"True," Dru said with a shrug, then her expression turned wistful. "But I wouldn't mind a dreamy stranger walking in off the street and sweeping me off my feet."

"Maybe if you worked less than eighty hours a week, you'd meet someone," Tasha said, and I knew she was right. We'd been so focused on building our business and following our dreams, that we'd forgotten to live our lives.

"Maybe it's time," I suggested as I sat up in the chair. "We've talked about making some of our part-time employee's full time, and hiring more part time. I know this is our baby and we've put everything we had into making it work. But, now that it *is* working, maybe we should loosen the reins a little and take some time to actually enjoy our success."

"I am enjoying it," Dru grumbled, sticking out her lower lip at the thought of having another person taking over the control that she held on to like a lifeline.

"I know you are, honey, but just think about how nice it would be to do something on a day other than Monday. Take in a movie, or maybe go on a dinner date . . ." I suggested, and knew I was busted again when her eyes narrowed on me.

"Mr. Adorable Dimples asked you out to dinner, didn't he?" she accused.

I nodded slowly.

"So, this isn't so much about *us* enjoying our lives, but about *you* fitting time into your busy schedule to get Dimples in the sack."

I could feel my face flush as I stammered, "No . . . uh, it's not that. You know I'm thinking of all of us, not . . . just me . . . and I don't want that . . . errr, at least, not yet."

"Calm down, Mills, you know she's just messing with you," Tasha said gently, shooting a glare at Dru, before admitting, "You and I both know she's right. It's time to grow a little bit and take a little time for ourselves. As much as we love what we're doing, we're all exhausted. Plus, if we had a full team, we'd have to turn away less clients. It's a win/win, Dru."

"I'll think about it," Dru said, which essentially meant she was giving in.

"Yay!" I cried, jumping from my chair and bounding over to lean down and hug my twin. "I'll talk to Claire about coming on full time when I ask her to cover for me Friday night."

Claire was my hardest working part-timer in the kitchen, and I knew she'd be a perfect sous chef. She was my first hope for a full-time employee.

"*This* Friday?" Tasha asked. "Where's he taking you?"

"Prime Beef," I replied, too happy to notice Tasha's scowl at the mention of the restaurant across the street. "I figured I can get almost everything done before four, then head upstairs to get ready and let Claire finish up. Then, maybe I'll ask Jackson up for dessert."

"Whoa!" Dru exclaimed, wiggling her eyebrows at me. "Dessert, huh?"

"Bow chica wow wow," Tasha sang, then started laughing.

"*Shut up*," I hissed, hating that I was blushing once again. I hated that I was so much more conservative and easily embarrassed than my sisters, even as a grown woman. "I mean *actual* dessert. I thought I'd make him my Lemon Crème Brule."

"One bite, and he'll never leave . . . I guar-an-tee," Dru said sweetly, allowing my subject change and having my back, as always.

Jackson

"Why do I have to go to Grandma's tonight? I want to stay home and play with Jess. I'll see them on Sunday." Kayla had been complaining since we got home from school, which had made trying to get her packed up, and myself ready for my date, extremely difficult.

I looked at my daughter, hoping what I was about to say next was the right thing. We didn't keep secrets from each other, unless it was something I thought she was too young to know, so I took in her scowling face and made a decision.

"Dad's got a date tonight, so Mama and Papa said they'd watch you. They said something about popcorn and movie night; I know you'll love that," I said, watching her closely as I spoke.

Because she had my undivided attention, I saw her scowl deepen and eyes narrow.

"A date?" she bit out, sounding more like Julie than ever.

"Yes, sweetheart, a date. I'm taking Millie out for dinner at Prime Beef."

"Millie, from my birthday party?" Kayla asked, her hands going to her hips as her lower lip jutted out in a pout.

"Yup, you liked her, remember?" I asked hopefully, not sure how to deal with this new version of my child.

"You can't go out with her . . . you're married, *remember*? Besides, I didn't like her. She's stupid."

"Kayla Ann Heeler," I warned, my voice low and firm. "You don't talk about people that way, and you certainly don't swear. Your mom has been gone for almost a year now, don't you think it's time for me to move on, have some fun, be happy?" I paused, hoping she'd give me something, but when she just kept scowling, I frowned at her and said, "We have to go, but we'll talk about your behavior later. Now, go get your bag and meet me at the car."

"*Whatever,*" my normally sweet, angelic girl said under her breath as she whirled and stomped off toward her room.

I stood there for a moment, watching after her and running a hand through my hair in frustration.

I deserve a little happiness, don't I? It's not the end of the world for a man to go on a date with a beautiful woman, enjoy some steak, and hopefully get to kiss her luscious lips again, right?

With a sigh, I turned to gather my things, then went to the door and paused, cocking my head to the side as I listened for movement.

When I didn't hear any, I bellowed, "Kayla, let's go!"

"Fine!" she shouted back, then I heard her door slam and her footsteps pounding down the hall as she came toward the door.

"You're really asking for it," I muttered as she moved past me and out the door.

She didn't reply, just got into the backseat and sunk low in the seat. I couldn't help but chuckle at her belligerence as I locked up and rounded my truck. Kayla only ever sat in the back seat when she was in a snit about something. It was one of her passive aggressive ways of letting me know she was mad at me.

I turned up the radio, since I knew the short drive would be filled with angry silence. When we arrived at her grandparents' house, Kayla jumped out and ran up the steps, disappearing into the house without saying goodbye.

I left the truck running, but got out to go say hello to my mother-in-law and let her know that Kayla was in a mood.

I knew she'd already figured that out when she stepped out onto the porch and asked, "What's up with Kayla?"

I waited until I was a few feet in front of her before replying gently, "I told her I was going on a date tonight."

The look on her face was sad, but understanding.

"I'll speak with her, Jackson," she said softly, then looked like she was trying to figure out what to say next, when she added, "It's time, son."

My heart clenched as the love I had for this woman filled me and I leaned in to give her a kiss on the cheek.

When I pulled back, I asked, "Have you heard from her?"

My mother-in-law shook her head sadly.

"I'm sorry, Ruth. I'm going to hire someone to find her, so I can get her served with divorce papers."

I watched her eyes fill and felt her pain right in my gut.

"Please," she whispered. "Let us know if you find her."

"I will, Ruth. Of course I will."

She nodded, wiped her cheeks, and managed a smile.

"I'll talk to Kayla, you go and have a good time. We'll see you tomorrow."

"Thanks, Ruth. Love you."

"Love you, too, Jackson," Ruth said, and I stood there until she shuffled back into the house and shut the door.

I hated Julie more in that moment than I had in months. I didn't understand how the woman that I'd known, the woman I'd married and had a child with, could turn out to be someone so totally different than I thought.

Pushing thoughts of Julie, Ruth, and Kayla from my mind, I got back in my truck and headed to Three Sisters Catering to pick up Millie. Although, Kayla and her unusual behavior kept inching its way back into my thoughts.

I prayed she wasn't still harboring hope of Julie coming home and us being a family again, but even as I thought it, I knew that was it, and my heart sank.

I'm going to have to break my daughter's heart all over again.

Fucking Julie.

Millie

I was watching by the window, without trying to *look* like I was. I didn't want to appear too eager, or like I was waiting for Jackson with my nose pressed against the glass of our storefront.

So, instead, I was half hiding behind the door to the back, watching like a creepy stalker.

I saw him pull up, park, and hop out of his truck. As he rounded the front, he wiped his palms against the side of his slacks, then pushed his glasses up his nose.

He's nervous.

I took a deep breath, a small smile playing on my lips, calm now that I knew he was feeling exactly the same way as I was, and walked fully out into the storefront and to the door.

Jackson's head came up as he caught my movement and he broke into a happy grin. He opened the door as I approached and held it so I could walk out past him. My arm brushed his hand as I passed, and I felt a tingle of anticipation run through me.

"Hi," I said softly, a little shyly.

"Hi," he replied, his tone also soft.

We stood there for a moment, on the sidewalk in front of my business, grinning at each other and taking the other in, then Jackson took my hand in his and brought it to his lips. When he brushed them against the back of my hand, my belly fluttered, and I allowed myself to enjoy every second of that moment.

"I can pick you up from your house," Jackson said, his hand still holding mine. "I didn't even think of it before, but I hope you didn't have to go home, then come back here to meet me."

"Actually, you are picking me up from home," I replied, a small laugh escaping unwittingly at his confused face as he looked back in through the window. "Upstairs," I clarified. "There are four studio apartments up there. Dru, Tasha, and I all live in them, and use the fourth for storage. They aren't big, but it works for us, at least for now."

"Oh, wow, that's pretty cool," Jackson said, his head falling back as he looked up at the window that led to my apartment. He brought his head back down to catch my eye and asked, "Are you hungry?"

"Starved," I admitted, and I was. I hadn't been able to eat lunch. I was too excited about the date, and wanted to make sure everything was done and Claire was fully briefed, so while I was out with Jackson, I could focus totally on us.

"Well, luckily, we only have to cross the street," Jackson said, gesturing jauntily toward Prime Beef, making me laugh at his silliness. He released my hand and crooked his elbow so I could tuck my arm though his. "Shall we?"

"Let's," I said with an exaggerated nod and a laugh.

We marched across the street, laughing the whole way. When we reached the entrance, Jackson paused and put a finger to his lips, then straightened up to full height and made a show of becoming serious.

One more laugh escaped me, but he shook his head with mock sternness. I nodded and did my best to put on a straight face as well.

I looked him over as I pulled myself together, and was struck by how handsome he was wearing dark slacks, a maroon button-down shirt, and a tie with small busts of Shakespeare decorating it. His hair was styled, but he had a small cowlick sticking out at the back, which only made him look more attractive somehow.

"Everything okay?" Jackson asked when he realized I was no longer playing along, but rather standing in front of the restaurant staring at him.

I felt my blush rise as I answered, "You look very handsome."

Jackson's eyes lit with pleasure, and he gave a half smile as he bent dramatically at the waist. When he straightened, he said, "And you, Millie, look gorgeous, although, you *always* look gorgeous. I'm sorry, I didn't say that right away. I was just so nervous, I forgot myself and started acting like a dork to cover my nerves."

I took a step closer to him, put my hand on his cheek, and assured him, "You're not a dork. I love your ability to have fun, be silly, wear a Shakespeare tie. I want you to feel comfortable with me and always be yourself. And, I'll let you in on a little secret . . . I was nervous too, and you calmed my nerves."

Jackson lowered his head, and my breath caught as I waited for his lips to touch mine. When they did, they did so only briefly, but oh, so sweetly. They brushed across mine once, then twice, before he pulled back slowly and smiled down at me.

"Ready?" he asked again, and I nodded somewhat dreamily, causing his smile to widen.

We shifted and he pulled open the door, then held it for me as we went inside.

Prime Beef was a classic steakhouse, with lots of rich wood, low lighting, and the beautiful sound of a saxophone playing throughout the room.

I hadn't eaten there before, since we never really had time, plus, anytime I'd seen the owner, he was scowling, so I'd never really had the urge to be a patron in his establishment. I had to admit though, if the food was anything like the décor, our experience was going to be fabulous.

I was beyond surprised to see the owner of Prime Beef, and the scowly face, walking toward us with a large grin, his hands outstretched.

"I thought I was going to have to call the fire department to turn the hose on you, Jacks," the tall, striking man said as he approached.

"Shut it," Jackson replied, taking his offered hand, then pulling him in for one of those man half-hug clap on the back things. "How've you been?"

"Pretty good, ready for football to start back up; you?"

"Great. School is good and Kayla is awesome," he replied, then he put his arm around my shoulder and said proudly, "And, *this* is Millie. Millie, this is Jericho, the owner of Prime Beef and my fantasy football nemesis."

"It's lovely to meet you, your restaurant is gorgeous," I gushed, holding out my hand.

Jericho turned to me, took me in, then his welcoming smile dropped. I guessed he wasn't a total jerk, because he did take my offered hand briefly, rather than leaving me hanging, but when he muttered, "One of the three sisters," and continued to look like he'd taken a bite of something rotten, I wondered what we'd done to earn that look.

Jackson

I don't know why Jericho's demeanor changed when he realized who Millie was, but I didn't like it one bit.

"Hey, brother, I'm not sure what just happened, but your tone, and your face, are kinda pissing me off," I warned, low enough so his employees couldn't hear me, but so that he definitely could.

Jericho's eyes shot to mine and he grimaced, then said sheepishly, "Sorry, man." Then, he turned his attention back to Millie took her hand back in his. "I apologize, Millie, it's very nice to meet you. Jackson is one of my great friends and I trust his judgement. I'm sorry for being rude."

Millie looked at him uncertainly, then asked softly, "You don't even know me, so why . . . ?"

Jericho looked over our heads, toward Three Sisters Catering.

"I know your sister, and let's just say, when things ended, they didn't end well. But, that has nothing to do with you, and I'm sorry for acting like an ass all this time. I'm happy to have you and Jackson and would love to take care of your dinner tonight."

"That won't be necessary," I replied, because, seriously, my first dinner date with Millie wasn't going to be *on the house*. I didn't use my friends that way, and I didn't want her to think I did. Plus, there was something about paying for her meal that made me feel good, like I was taking care of her . . . If that made me old-fashioned, so be it.

"My sister?" Millie asked, still stuck on Jericho's explanation.

"She should tell it," Jericho said with a wave of his hand, and I knew he was done talking about it. He turned and held his hand out toward the dining room. "I have your table ready, if you'll follow me."

I shot a smile at the hostess as we passed, taking Millie's hand as we followed Jericho through the dining room, to a rounded booth in the back corner. I'd called ahead and told Jericho I was bringing a date. Since he was my friend, and happy that I was finally moving on from Julie, Jericho promised a romantic evening.

I let Millie's hand go so that we could both slide in, meeting each other in the middle on the other side. I smiled, liking that she chose to sit next to me, rather than across, although the brush of her thigh against mine might make focusing on my meal difficult.

"Ky will be your server tonight, but don't hesitate to call if you need anything," Jericho told us, then gave us a slight nod before walking off toward the kitchen.

"That was weird," Millie muttered as she watched Jericho push through the swinging door.

"Yeah, I've never seen him act like that; he's usually really easy going. Do you know what it's about?"

Millie shook her head, then turned it toward me.

"No, I mean, I thought maybe he didn't like us moving in and being competition, even though we really aren't, or that he was just a grumpy guy."

"He's not."

"Strange . . . And, now, I'm dying to know if he was talking about Tasha or Dru, and why whoever it is never said anything." Millie shook her head again, then smiled sweetly up at me. "Enough about them, that's a puzzle to figure out later. How was the rest of your week?"

"Great, the kids are diving in to *Pride and Prejudice*, which always brings about the best discussions."

"Oh, I love *Pride and Prejudice*," she gushed, her face taking on that dreamy quality that always came up when women thought of Darcy. "And, Kayla, how's she doing?"

"It's nice of you to ask," I said, wondering if I should tell her about Kayla's behavior earlier, or allow us the opportunity to get to know each other better, before weighing her down with my parenting woes. I decided on the latter and simply said, "She always loves spending time with her grandparents."

"Good," she said as she picked up the menu and opened it. "So, I've never been here, but I've heard great things. Is there anything you'd recommend?"

"Well, they make a mean martini, you can't go wrong with the steaks, and the dessert . . ." I put my fingertips up to my lips and kissed them. "*Magnifique*."

I noticed her cheeks get red, and couldn't help but be charmed when I learned why.

"Actually, I thought I'd have you back to my place for dessert. I made a Lemon Crème Brule that I think you'll enjoy."

My heart hammered in my chest at the thought of going back to her place, first with excitement, then with nerves.

Is she expecting more than dessert after dinner? Are we ready for that? Am I?

Not only had I never kissed anyone other than Julie, I'd never *been with* anyone other than her, and it had been well over a year since we'd had sex . . . since *I'd* had sex. I was a little rusty, and had never felt more inexperienced than I did in that moment just thinking about being alone with Millie in her apartment.

It's only the first date, I assured myself. There was no way Millie was thinking about taking things that far.

But when I looked at her pretty pink cheeks, and the way her lips were slightly parted as she watched my reaction play over my face, I wondered if I was not only being old-fashioned, but naïve.

"It's just dessert," Millie assured me softly, placing her soft, warm hand on my thigh in what she meant to be a reassuring gesture, but made me jump in me seat. She pulled her hand away quickly, as if she'd been burned and muttered, "Sorry."

I immediately felt guilty and reached for her hand, putting it back on my leg.

"No, I'm sorry, I'm overreacting and all you're doing is being sweet. I got nervous," I admitted, squeezing her hand slightly in mine. "I freaked out at the thought of what you might be expecting at the end of this date, which is unfair to you. As I've said, I'm out of practice with all of this stuff, and it's making me a bit of the mess."

"Hey," she said, leaning in to bump my arm with her shoulder. "I just thought it would be nice to have some dessert, with wine . . . *or coffee*, at my place so that we could have some privacy and get to know each other better. That's it." Her face lit up as she smiled a bit wickedly, then added, "I won't jump your bones, promise."

I chuckled, embarrassed, and had no control over my body's reaction to Millie's words. As my body tightened and a yearning filled me, I wondered whether I actually wanted to her keep that promise, or not.

Fifteen

Millie

"Does it feel like you never get a break, working and living in the same building?" Jackson asked as we walked across the street.

Dinner had been perfect. Delicious food, easy conversation, and no more weird run-ins with Jericho. Now, we were on our way to my place for dessert and all of my earlier bravado had left me. I thought it was terribly sweet that Jackson was nervous about being alone in my apartment and what my expectations may be, and at first, I'd assured him easily that there was nothing to be nervous about.

Then, over the course of dinner, my mind kept circling back to our conversation, and my nerves had grown. It wasn't that I was worried that he was anticipating a certain ending, I knew he wasn't, but my fear had grown from something else . . . Him. I liked him so much, and everything about him, about us, seemed to fit so perfectly, what if I somehow ruined it?

Maybe I should cut the night off now, before I have the chance to screw things up. End on a happy note . . .

But, as I looked from our swinging hands to Jackson's open,

friendly face, I knew I didn't want to cut our time short. In fact, I wanted to lock him away in my apartment and never let him go.

Okay, maybe that is too far, but still.

"Um, no, not really," I replied, finally answering his question. "It's nice to be close to my sisters again, but still have my own space to disappear to when I need to be alone. Plus, it made our lives easier, starting out, to be so close to work."

"I bet," Jackson conceded as I opened the door. "But, what about now? Now that your business is up and running? Do you think you'll stay here?"

"Yeah, sure, at least for now." I locked up behind us, then led him up the stairs to the living areas. "I mean, that may change when one of us gets serious with someone, decides to start a family, or gets tired of apartment life. This isn't where any of us plan to live forever, but it's worked our perfectly so far."

We passed Dru's door, then Tasha's, before we came to mine, which was across from the empty apartment we used for storage.

"This is it," I said unnecessarily, my hands shaking slightly as I put the key in and turned. I opened the door, then stepped back and gestured for him to go inside.

As Jackson walked in, I stepped in behind him and closed the door, then followed his gaze, seeing my apartment through his eyes.

I'd made an effort to clean before I got dressed, so it looked tidy, if not sparkling. My gray sofa was made up with throw pillows and a blanket that I liked to snuggle under when watching TV. I had two mirrors over the couch as accent pieces, in an effort to make the small space seem bigger. My kitchen was small, but cute, with a shelf over the sink that held some of my favorite display cases, with my pans hanging on hooks underneath.

I'd mostly decorated in pinks, grays, and white, and liked my décor on the feminine side. I thought it suited me, and I loved coming home to it every night.

"Uh . . ." Jackson began, and I tore my gaze from my throw pillows to see him standing in front of the built-ins that surrounded my TV. "Is there something you want to tell me?"

I flushed slightly, but kept my tone free of embarrassment when I said sternly, "No, why? Don't you like The King of Rock 'n Roll?"

Jackson shifted toward me, eyes mockingly wide, then turned back and flung his arm out at my Elvis collection.

"I like Elvis as much as the next guy, but I'm guessing you're not *the next guy*. There seems to be a bit of an obsession going on here."

My built-ins displayed my most prized possessions. Elvis plates, dolls, pez dispensers, metal wall hangings, video tapes, DVDs, original magazines, posters, and the crowning jewel, a guitar with case.

"I've loved Elvis ever since I saw *Blue Hawaii* with my mom as a little girl. I've seen all of his movies, numerous times, his concerts . . . on video, of course, and have all of his records. It's become a running joke in my family. Every birthday, Christmas, shoot, *any* holiday, everyone gets me Elvis-themed gifts. These," I said, holding my hand out to my built-ins, "are just some of my favorite pieces. I have boxes and boxes full of stuff."

Not to mention the poodle skirt in my drawer and the Elvis canvas shoes in my closet . . .

"So, any guy that gets serious with you, has to be prepared to accept Elvis into their lives?" Jackson joked, stepping close and putting his arms around me.

I tilted my head back as he pulled me close, the smile playing on his lips doing funny things to my insides.

"That is correct," I replied, then snuggled in even closer and whispered against his lips, "And maybe wear a Hawaiian shirt and tight board shorts once in a while."

"I think I can handle that," he murmured, then lowered his mouth to mine.

I sighed into the kiss, happy to be in Jackson's arms again. It was like we had all the time in the world; there was no fervor or impatience to this kiss, only time, attention, and plenty of thoroughness.

By the time Jackson broke the kiss and straightened, I was practically boneless in his arms, ready to say and do anything he wanted. Of course, after our discussion at dinner, I knew he wanted to take things slow; my body, however, was warring with my mind after that kiss.

Maybe if I offer to give him a tour of my bedroom, he'll take the hint, I thought. Instead, I tiptoed up to brush my lips against his one more time, before asking, "Would you like wine or coffee with your Crème Brule?"

"Wine," Jackson replied, his eyes just a bit mischievous, which I hoped would lead to *at least* some making out on my couch later.

Jackson

It may not be manly to admit, although I've never been afraid of my softer side, but after my evening with Millie, I was floating on a cloud.

The date had gone better than I imagined. Aside from Jericho's bizarre behavior, the evening had been perfect.

I loved getting to know Millie better. Her close relationship with her sisters, her random Elvis obsession, and the way her lips met mine eagerly after a delicious helping of Lemon Crème Brule and a glass of wine, all only further fueled my desire to spend time with her.

I was in danger of acting like my students. Utterly lovesick and impossible to be around. And, I loved it.

After a night of deep, soundless sleep, I awoke feeling refreshed and excited, already counting the minutes until I'd get to see Millie again. Only one black cloud overshadowed my happiness, the fact that today was the day I started the search for Julie.

Would it take days, weeks, or God forbid months? I had no idea, all I knew was that it was time to sever the tie that held me to what had become a destructive force in my life.

With Kayla safely tucked away with her grandparents, I spent my morning straightening up, then made my way out of town to the neighboring county, where the P.I. my buddy Rob had recommended set up business.

I pulled up to the nondescript building just shy of noon, my appointment time, and took a deep breath before going inside.

I was about to change the course of our lives forever, mine and Kayla's. Or, at least, I was about to complete the changes that Julie had initiated when she walked out. It felt like a defining moment, while at the same time like realizing the inevitable.

There was no jingle when the door opened, no secretary waiting to greet me and offer me coffee, and no charming, quaintly decorated office waiting to welcome new clients.

No, Michael "Mick" O'Donnelly's office looked more like a man cave than an office.

With dark, rich leather sofas and a recliner facing a large, flat-screen TV, a mini fridge on the wall next to a fully stocked bar, and a dartboard in the corner, I almost turned around and went out to check the address on the building, sure I'd just walked into someone's house, rather than an office.

But, past the kick-ass lounge area, there was an office. Huge oak desk, three filing cabinets, five bookshelves, and a large, Irish guy sitting behind a computer, typing away.

"You Heeler?" the man asked without looking up from his task. His voice was deep and gruff, and as I crossed through the living space to get to one of the empty chairs sitting in front of the desk, I was surprised to see that he was around my age.

I guess I read too many books, watched too many movies, because nothing about this private investigator was what I'd been expecting.

"Yeah, Jackson," I replied, and once I was in reaching distance, I stuck out my hand in greeting. "You can call me Jacks."

"Mick," he said, giving my hand one quick, firm shake, before resuming his typing. "Have a seat. I just gotta finish up this summary while things are fresh in my mind. There's water and beer in the fridge, if you want."

"I'm good."

I sat in the chair closest to me, immediately thinking that I needed to find out where Mick had bought it and get one for my classroom. It was that comfortable.

My eyes darted around the office space as I tried not to awkwardly stare at the man in front of me. He was big; like, even sitting, I could tell the dude was mammoth. Probably did that CrossFit workout, which I would totally do if I had time, and didn't have the upper body strength of a ten-year-old.

He was a contrast of light and dark. Pale skin, with dark hair and eyebrows, but when his eyes had met mine, I'd been startled by how light green they were. I'd never seen eyes that color, they were pretty cool.

Of course, I wouldn't tell him that . . . The guy would probably toss me like a tire if I commented on his cool eye color.

The typing stopped and Mick started talking.

"Right, so on the phone you stated this is a missing persons case. Can you give me more details?"

Mick leaned back in his chair, it was the kind that moved when you reclined, and crossed his hands over his stomach, those light-green eyes pinning me in place.

It was a little unnerving.

"Uh, yeah, well, not *missing* so much as walked out and left. My wife walked out almost a year ago, saying she needed to *not* be a wife and mother anymore. We were smothering her, holding her back, and she needed to go find herself. I haven't heard from her since."

"What about her family?"

I shook my head.

"No, they said they haven't heard from her either, and I believe them. We're close. They're close with my parents, and we see each other all the time. My daughter is with them right now, in fact, and my mother-in-law asked me to let them know if you find Julie."

"Are you sure they're telling the truth, not just keeping a promise to their daughter?"

"Yeah, no, I know they're telling the truth. Ruth, my mother-in-law, had not only lost weight in the past year, she's lost a bit of her shine, ya know? Julie's disappearing act had taken a toll on her . . . She doesn't know where she is."

Mick gave one sharp nod and sat up, reaching for a pad of paper and sliding it toward me. He laid a pen on top and ordered, "Write down the names of everyone you can think of who knew her, don't leave anyone out. Co-workers, friends, family, the guy who mowed your lawn . . . everyone. I'll start there, then follow the trail."

"You think you can find her?" I looked at the man who could finally put this Chapter of my life to rest, and realized I believed he actually could.

"Never failed before," Mick claimed. "Don't plan on it now."

And that is good enough for me.

Millie

"We totally rocked that reception," Dru said happily as she leaned her head back and closed her eyes, champagne flute in hand.

We'd had one of the rare events where all hands were needed on deck, so the three of us, along with all of our staff, had spent all day and all evening on Sunday pulling off our biggest wedding reception yet.

A lot of blood, sweat, and tears had gone into making it come off seamlessly. But it was all worth it.

Now that everything had been cleaned up and torn down, my sisters and I were back at our building, sitting in the quiet dining area out front. The shutters were drawn, so no one could see in, and it was blissfully peaceful.

"Yeah, we did," Tasha replied, raising her glass and nudging Dru with her knee to get her to sit up and open her eyes. "To Three Sisters, us, and the business, for becoming more than I ever imagined. Great job tonight."

My feet were throbbing and my lower back niggled, but I wore a huge smile as I clinked my glass to theirs.

"To Three Sisters."

I sipped my champagne with a happy sigh, enjoying the feel of the bubbles sliding down my throat.

"It was a successful day," I said as I moved my head back and forth to get the kinks out of my neck. "But, I sure am glad we're off tomorrow."

"Amen," Dru replied, then narrowed her eyes at me and said, "We've been so busy, I haven't had a chance to get the deets from Friday night."

"Oh, yeah," Tasha cooed as she scooted her chair closer and leaned over the table toward me, resting her chin in her hands and blinking slowly at me.

"Stop," I said with a laugh as I gently pushed at her head.

Tasha slapped at my hand and ordered, "Spill. Now. You know we are living vicariously through you. Don't leave anything out . . . Is he rough or gentle? Bottom or top? Does he talk dirty, or recite lines from one of his romance novels? C'mon, tell all."

"Geez," Dru said with a snort. "I don't really want *that* much information about Millie's sex life, I just want to know which base they hit. You need a night out, Tash."

"I know," Tasha sighed dramatically, and we all laughed. "But seriously, Mills, how did it go?"

"Dinner was delicious, and so was dessert," I began coyly, then I remembered the incident at Prime Beef and decided it was time to turn the tables on them for once. "To answer your question, Dru, we got to second . . . and all I'll say, Tasha, is *yes*, to everything you asked."

"*Oh*," Tasha said, her eyes wide and her mouth forming an O.

"Now, I have a question for you guys," I said, sharpening my gaze on both my sisters as I looked to each of them to catch their reactions. "*Jericho Smythe.*"

I watched the blood drain from Tasha's face. *Bingo.*

After a beat, Dru said, "Ah, that's not a question, it's a name . . . Who's Jericho Smythe?"

"Ask Tasha," I said, my eyes never leaving our younger sister's face.

Dru turned her head toward Tasha and asked, "Who's Jericho Smythe?"

When Tasha didn't answer, I said, "The owner of Prime Beef. Apparently, there's some history between our brooding neighbor and our little sis."

"*What*?" Dru practically screeched. I could understand her shock, we had been working across from Jericho for well over a year, commenting on how grumpy he always seemed and wondering why he seemed to hate us, and all this time, Tasha had been the reason. It was too bizarre.

"*Apparently*," I started when it appeared Tasha was going to remain mute. "They were together and it ended badly. Like, together, together."

"*What*?" Dru screeched again, obviously unable to form complete sentences.

"The question I had was, *when*, but after thinking about it, it became obvious," I stated, watching as pain flitted across Tasha's face. I gentled my voice and asked, "It was when you were at college, wasn't it? Before Mom got sick."

Tasha nodded slowly, and my heart hurt when a tear slid down her cheek.

"Oh my gosh, it was serious," Dru said, finally finding her words and scooting over to put her arm around Tasha. "What happened?"

"We were in love," Tasha said softly, her voice rough as if she'd been crying for hours.

I reached my hand out over the table to place it over hers and squeeze gently.

She took a deep breath and added, "When I met Jericho, it was like being hit by lightning. He was so . . . *everything*. Handsome, confident, *sexy*. He was in my accounting class, a few years ahead of me in school, and seemed to have it all together. I was young, it was my first time out on my own, and I felt like a total fish out of water. I kept wondering what I was doing there, and even had the urge to drop out and come home, then he asked me out for coffee."

Tasha laughed, as if still unable to believe the handsome, older man wanted to ask her out, her face lighting briefly before it fell.

"It was a whirlwind; he became everything to me, so much so that it scared the crap out of me. He's pretty intense, and always knew exactly what he wanted, whereas I was still trying to figure it all out. Not him, I mean, I was certain I was in love with him . . . head over heels. But, I was unsure of what I wanted to do with my life, and I craved my independence. You guys know that, that's why I left, and I began to worry that I was losing my will to gain that independence, because I was so enamored with Jericho."

When Tasha fell silent, Dru pushed, "And, then?"

"Then, Mom got sick. Millie had finished culinary school, and you were on your last semester. I knew I needed to be here with you guys, and with Mom, so I decided to come back home and transfer . . . finish school here."

"And, Jericho?" I asked softly.

Tasha hung her head, and her voice was so low, I had to strain to hear her response.

"I just left. I was a complete coward, and took Mom's sickness as a sign that I needed to break away from Jericho and figure out what *I* wanted out of life." Tasha lifted her head, the tears flowing freely now. "He's right to hate me. I've been waiting for him to confront me, to tell me off, or scream at me, but he hasn't. He's ignored me . . . all this time . . . as if I meant nothing. As if I didn't break both of our hearts by walking away. And, I guess maybe I didn't. Maybe he didn't even notice I was gone."

With that, Tasha stood up and walked out. Dru's eyes sought mine, and I knew what she was thinking . . . We needed to kick Jericho Smythe's ass.

Jackson

Hey! I know you have school, but can you break away for lunch? If not, it's totally okay. Just thought I'd ask.

I was walking down the hall, the discussion my class had just had on the pros and cons of Mr. Darcy still playing in my mind, when Millie's text came through. An instant grin and, I'm a little embarrassed to say, some stomach flutters, were my immediate reaction to seeing her name pop up on my phone.

Unfortunately, I didn't have time to break away during the school day, but was so pleased that Millie contacted me and wanted to see me, that I wondered just how strict Principal Wiggins' policy on non-staff members eating in the lounge was . . .

Realizing I was willing to risk it, I texted back:

Can't break free for lunch, but you could come here. I'll even share my peanut butter and banana sandwich. My break is until 12:30.

I was standing in the middle of the hallway, looking down at my phone as I awaited Millie's reply, when a gentle hand on my shoulder, and softly spoken, "Jackson?" shook me out of my revere and had me looking up.

"Oh, hey, Rebecca. Sorry, I didn't see you there," I replied sheepishly, then looked back down when I felt the phone vibrate in my hand.

Lol, I won't steal your sandwich, I'll bring my own. Should I go to the front office?

No, I'll meet you at the side of the school, just follow the sign that says staff parking and I'll be there.

"Uh, sorry, Rebecca," I muttered as I tore my gaze from my phone and back to her. "What's up?"

My phone vibrated again.

Perfect, see you in ten.

"If this is a bad time . . ." Rebecca began, her voice trailing off as I turned my attention to her once more and placed my phone in my back pocket.

"Sorry, no, of course not," I said, then felt a stab of panic in my chest. What if what Ty had said was true, and Rebecca was about to ask me out?

I noticed she was wringing her hands nervously and that her eyes kept darting around the hall, looking at everyone and everything but me.

"Well, this may be weird, but I was wondering . . ."

When she paused, I placed a reassuring hand on her shoulder and squeezed gently.

"Rebecca, I think you're great. I've loved getting to know you over the years, and having you by my side at the dances always make them much easier to bear, but I think of you as a friend . . ."

Rebecca looked from my hand on her shoulder to my face, her own looking quite puzzled.

"Huh?" she asked, and a different kind of dread began to fill me. *The embarrassing, mortifying kind.*

"You weren't going to ask me out?" I asked cautiously, even though I could tell by the look on her face that she wasn't. "I'm sorry, it's just, I'm seeing someone, and Ty said you had a crush on me . . ."

Rebecca's mouth formed a small O, and she smacked the heel of her hand to her forehead.

"That explains it," she sighed.

"What?"

"Last year, after Julie, I may have had a small crush," Rebecca began, holding her finger and thumb up to indicate just how small.

"Not necessary," I muttered, pushing her hand down with mine and looking around us in hopes that no one else had heard our conversation, or misunderstood what she'd been indicating was small.

"*But*, after spending time with you, and being your shoulder afterwards, I realized that we were *definitely* more suited to be friends." As I was trying to process whether or not that hurt my feelings, she continued, "And, since then, I've come to realize who I really have feelings for, and was worried that I had no shot, but now it all makes sense, because he thinks I'm into you."

It took me a moment to brush off my feelings and catch up, and when I did, I cried, "*Ty?*"

Rebecca grimaced at my reaction, smoothed her hand over her hair in what I knew was a nervous gesture, and said, "Look, I know he's kind of a *player*, but, I really, *really* like him. He's smart, funny, a great teacher, and totally hot."

This time I grimaced. What were we now, *gossip buddies*? I didn't want to hear how *hot* one of my friends thought my other friend was . . . In fact, now that I knew I was off the hook, I wanted to get the heck out of this conversation and go wait for Millie.

"Ah, *look*, Rebecca," I began, but she stopped me.

"Jackson, I just want you to feel him out, see if he's interested, and maybe . . . put in a good word?"

She looked so hopeful that I couldn't say anything but, "Yes. Of course I will, but I gotta run, okay?"

"Okay," Rebecca said with a big grin, then bounced up on her toes and gave me a kiss on the cheek and added, "You're the best."

I chuckled as she practically skipped down the hall, then turned and rushed to meet Millie at the side door. I could see her walking up the sidewalk through the window of the door as I approached. She was loaded down with her purse, a stylish lunch bag, and a large container that I really hoped contained a cake.

I opened the door and held it for her, her smile warming me when she looked up and saw me standing there.

"Hey," Millie said sweetly as she brushed passed me. She lifted her arms a fraction and added, "I brought a red velvet cake."

My response was to sigh and say, *"I love you."*

Nineteen

Millie

I stopped walking once I realized I was marching down the hall alone and had no idea where I was going. I turned to see Jackson still standing at the door, frozen, his mouth gaping a bit as he moved it but no sound came out.

I tried to figure out what had happened, then his words came back to me and I guffawed.

"Calm down, Jackson, I know it was just a reaction to the cake, and you don't actually love me," I assured him, even though the words had given me a quick thrill coming out of his mouth. "You're such a nervous Nelly. People tell me they love me all the time after they get a taste of my cooking."

Relief filled his face and he smiled as he crossed to me.

"Really? I have a lot of competition, huh?"

"Yup," I quipped, matching his step as we made our way down the empty hallway.

It was kind of weird being in a high school again. Brought back memories. Some good, like me and Dru laughing as we rushed through the halls to get to soccer practice before we got busted by

Coach. Or bad, like the time my boyfriend Cooper told me he was breaking up with me to go out with the head cheerleader.

"Did you just call me a *nervous Nelly*?" Jackson asked, his voice filled with mirth, pulling me out of my thoughts.

"I sure did," I replied with a chuckle. "You keep getting caught in your head about things you're worried I think or expect, and I totally get it, you're out of your element and it throws you off. But, Jackson, I'm really enjoying being with you, and I hope you're enjoying being with me too. I'm not putting pressure on either of us, and if you get nervous or wonder what I'm thinking or feeling, just ask, okay? I promise I'll tell you."

Jackson stopped and smiled down at me, then bent to brush his lips softly against mine.

"*All right*, Mr. H!"

We jumped apart and I flushed, then we grinned at each other and he took the cake out of my hands.

"Sorry, I should have grabbed this right away. C'mon."

I looked around the teacher's lounge as we entered, and it looked exactly how I always imagined one would look. Full coffee pot and microwave on the counter, a large fridge, and about five round tables scattered throughout the room. There was a small, flat-screen TV off to one side, and it was currently turned to a morning talk show.

There were about eight women scattered throughout and two men sitting at a table at the back of the room. One was a little older, and a little rounder, with light-brown hair and kind eyes, while the other was obviously physically fit, with close-cropped black hair, toffee-colored skin, and a face made to flirt. Their heads had come up when Jackson opened the door, and they tracked our progress through the room.

"Guys, this is Millie," Jackson said as we came to a stop at their table. He sounded like he was proud to be introducing me to them, which warmed me from within, and I had to hold back a snort at the way they kept looking between us, silent, their eyes wide. "Millie, these mutes are my buddies. Rob teaches Algebra One and Ty, PE and Health."

"It's nice to meet you both," I said, thinking Rob looked exactly like the algebra teacher I'd had in high school, and that Ty probably had his hands full with hormonal teenaged girls who thought their gym teacher was hot.

"She brought us cake," Jackson added, lifting the cake an inch as proof, when his friends still didn't respond.

"Red velvet," I offered, and they finally shook off their shock.

"Red velvet? My favorite, don't tell Jan," Rob joked before taking a sip of coke.

I assumed Jan was his wife and said, "I promise."

Ty stood up and offered me a hand, which I shook, then gestured toward the chair and said, "Please, sit. Sorry we lost it for a minute there, we thought Jackson was exaggerating when he said how beautiful you are and were struck when we realized he'd been holding back."

I laughed as Jackson rolled his eyes and went to set the cake down on the counter.

"That's very sweet, Ty, thank you," I said, my cheeks warming. "I know you don't have a long break for lunch. Thanks for letting me join you."

"Believe me, it's our pleasure," Ty responded smoothly.

"All right, all right," Jackson chided as he sat. "That's enough, smooth talker."

Ty looked mock offended, then sat back, grinned, and popped some almonds in his mouth.

"I'm sorry, we only have ten minutes left, is that even enough time for you to eat?" Jackson asked, leaning in so that our shoulders brushed.

I looked up at him and found myself lost in his eyes for a moment. I noticed flecks of green in the brown, which seemed to twinkle behind his glasses, and I bit back a sigh as I remember how they'd looked when he'd gazed down at me Friday night when we were laying on my couch.

His dimple popped out and he murmured, "Millie?"

"Hmm?" I realized I was staring and turned my attention to my lunch bag. I pulled out my sandwich and chanced a peek up, only to see Rob and Ty grinning at me like crazy. I flushed and said, "*Hi.*"

"Hi," they replied in unison, still grinning, and I heard Jackson chuckle next to me.

"You know, Millie, we're so happy to meet you, really. Jackson's had such a hard time since Julie, and it's nice to see him looking happier than I ever have," Rob said.

"*Rob,*" Jackson warned, probably not wanting Julie brought up, but Rob ignored his warning.

"*What*? It's the truth, and Millie should know."

"We're going out on Saturday night, you should come with us," Ty invited.

"Where are you going?" I asked, even though I had to work and it would be impossible take another weekend night off. Still, it was nice of them to invite me.

"Well, Rob likes country bars, and Ty likes to go out dancing, so we always go to the Irish pub. Kind of meet in the middle."

"I don't know if an Irish pub is in the middle of a dance club and a country bar, but it works out. Pretty low key, so we can hang out and have a few drinks," Ty added.

"That sounds like a lot of fun, and I wish I could, but we have two events on Saturday, and there's no way I can miss it. Maybe next time?"

"Ah, that's right, you're a business owner . . . Do you get any days off?" Rob asked.

"We're off Mondays."

"Next Monday is a Teacher Work Day. We could change our plans to Sunday night, would that work?" Ty asked, and I thought it was really sweet that they wanted me there on their guys night.

"Um," I mentally flipped through our calendar. "Yes, actually, Sunday's event is a brunch, so should be done and cleaned up by four."

"Let's do that then," Ty said, then paused, grinned and asked, "Didn't Jackson say you have sisters?"

"Ty," Jackson said, trying to sound chastising, but ruining it when he laughed at his friend.

"What? I'm just sayin', they deserve a night out, right? Why not all meet up and have dinner and drinks."

"I'll see if Jan wants to come," Rob added, then frowned and said, "Of course then I can't have beer or corned beef. Maybe I won't invite Jan."

"I'll talk to my sisters, see if they want to go," I said with a laugh.

"Perfect," Jackson said, and I turned to him and smiled, happy at the prospect of another night out with him, even if it was in a group.

Just then, the bell rang, and Jackson muttered, "Shoot, you didn't even get a bite of your sandwich."

"It's okay," I promised as I rose to my feet. "I had fun."

Jackson leaned down and I rose up, eager to meet his lips, but before we touched, a stern voice said, "Mr. Heeler," and we both jumped back.

We turned our heads slowly to see a short man wearing a button up, tie, and scowl.

"Who's that?" I whispered.

"Principal," Jackson replied, then said, "Go, I'll deal with him."

I gathered my things and hurried out.

As I was leaving, I heard Rob say, "That cake better still be here after school," the principal ask, "Who was that? You weren't having a date during school hours, were you, Mr. Heeler?" and Ty urge, "Give the guy a break, Wiggins, he's finally happy." Then I got out of there as fast as I could.

Jackson

It had been a few days since I'd gotten chewed out by Wiggins for having a date in the teacher's lounge, the thought of which still made me smile. I'd pointed out to the principal that there was no actual written rule about such a thing, to which he'd huffed that it was implied, and asked if I'd ever seen anyone else have guests over for lunch.

Although I had seen Jan on occasion when Rob had forgotten his lunch, I'd known I was toeing the line by inviting Millie. The thing was, I couldn't find it in me to care. I hadn't seen her since, and that was four days ago, so I was happy that I'd gotten to see her, even if it was only for a few minutes.

We'd been mostly keeping in touch by texting each other throughout the day. We'd talked a few times, but we were on different schedules, and she was usually still working when I got off. I'd always heard owning your own business was tough, but the amount of hours Millie and her sisters put in was staggering.

Luckily, they were talking about hiring more full-time work. I didn't know how they'd been functioning for over a year and was happy they were in a place where they could bring on more help and give themselves a bit of a break.

I shook my head and looked back down at the papers I was grading. This had been happening a lot lately, me daydreaming about Millie when I was supposed to be doing something else. There was no denying, the woman was getting under my skin.

The thought had me smiling as I focused on the paper in front of me.

The students had grumbled when they'd walked into class and found a pop quiz of sorts waiting on their desks. But, it was less of a quiz than a chance for them to give me their opinions on what we'd been reading and discussing in class. It helped me determine how much they'd comprehended the material, while giving me insight into their thoughts and feelings on the subject.

I did this with each book we read, and it was one of my favorite parts of the class, seeing how one work could be interpreted in so many different ways.

"Daddy?"

I looked across the table to where Kayla was doing her homework.

"Yeah, sweetheart?"

"Do I have to go stay with Mama and Papa again this weekend?" she asked, avoiding my eyes as she played with her pencil.

I set the red pen I was holding down on the paper and adjusted my glasses as I looked at my daughter with concern.

"You love staying with them. Did something happen? Is there a reason why you don't want to go over there?"

Kayla shrugged one shoulder and still didn't look at me.

"Kayla," I spoke softly, encouragingly. "What's going on, honey?"

"It's just no fun over there anymore," she whispered. "Mama's always sad, and Papa's always angry."

I sighed, mentally berating Julie for the negative effect she was having on everyone's lives, even a year later.

"They don't mean anything by it, they're just missing your mom."

"I know, but it makes me sad to be there."

"Do you want me to talk to Grandma and see if you can stay with her and Grandpa?" I asked, talking about my parents.

Kayla shook her head.

"Do you want me to stay home? I was going to meet up with Rob and Ty, as well as Millie and her sisters, who I haven't met yet." I watched Kayla's face pinch at the mention of Millie, but I wasn't going to hide my relationship from my daughter. She'd have to come to terms with it eventually. "I could have Millie come here instead, and we could hang out. It would give you the chance to get to know her better."

Kayla's head popped up and she said, "No, that's okay. I mean, I don't want you to miss out on your friends. I was thinking, maybe we could ask Jess's mom if I could stay over there. There's no school on Monday, so . . ."

And, there it was . . .

I had no doubt that Julie's parents were having a hard time adjusting to Julie's disappearing act, but the real reason why Kayla didn't want to go there was because she wanted to be with her friends. I guess at nine, she was getting to the point where hanging out with her grandparents all the time wasn't as exciting as it used to be.

I've been played.

"You could have just come out and asked me about staying with Jess, you know."

Kayla watched me closely, probably trying to figure out if I was angry or not, then sighed and asked, "So, you really like this Millie person?"

I got up, walked around the table, and crouched down in front of my daughter.

"Yeah, Kayla, I really like her. You have to know that things with your mom and me are through, and after all this time, and the way she left, that's never going to change."

I watched her face fall as my words sank in and her eyes filled up.

"I'll always love her for giving me you, but it's time for me to move on. I know you aren't thrilled about me dating Millie, but I hope you'll give her a chance. I'll call Jess's mom and go out, and we won't have her over this weekend, but, Kayla, I do want to do something, just the three of us, soon, okay?"

Kayla frowned, but nodded slowly, and I knew it wasn't going to be easy, and she probably wouldn't welcome Millie with open arms, but at least it was a start.

"Okay, how about we finish up here, then order pizza, pop some popcorn, and catch up on *Fuller House*?"

Kayla grinned, because she knew I hated *Fuller House* almost as much as she loved it, and said, "Yay!"

Millie

"I'm so excited that we're doing this," I said as my sisters and I drove to O'Reilly's, the Irish pub.

The event had run a little longer than expected, which happens more often than you might think, so I'd texted Jackson and told him I'd ride with Dru and Tasha and meet him there. It gave us the rare opportunity to get ready to go out together, something that didn't happen as much anymore, and I'd forgotten how much fun it was.

We'd "pre-gamed" with Dru's blackberry margaritas, and done each other's hair while trying on different outfits. It reminded me of when we were younger. The only thing missing was our mother sitting in the corner laughing as we paraded through the room in our different outfits.

"Me, too," Dru admitted. "I can't remember the last time I went out to a bar."

"Yeah, it's been a minute," Tasha agreed. Her bright-red hair was down in pretty, beachy waves, and she was wearing a simple, but sexy, black dress.

"I'm a little nervous about you guys meeting Jackson, though. Promise you'll go easy?" I asked, mostly talking to Dru. I knew Tasha would go in with an open mind and be nice, but Dru was a wild card.

"Who, me?" Dru asked with mock offense, which made me groan.

"Yes, you, dear sister. I want you to go into this thinking you're going to like him, instead of expecting to hate him, like you've done with everyone else I've dated."

"In my defense, everyone else you've dated has been an idiot . . . You can't really blame me for that."

I shut my eyes, shook my head, and wondered if I should just jump out of the car now . . . save myself the embarrassment.

"Relax, Mills," Dru cajoled, and I opened my eyes to look at her almost identical ones. "Everything you've told us about him makes him sound pretty great. I'll give him a shot, all right?"

Of course, as soon as we walked in and joined Jackson, Ty, Rob, and who I assumed was Rob's wife Jan, Dru walked right up to Jackson and asked, "So, have you unloaded the wife yet?"

"*Dru*," I hissed as I grabbed her arm, then looked to Jackson, face flushed, and said, "Sorry."

Jackson just laughed and stood, then shocked my twin when he wrapped his arms around Dru.

"It's great to finally meet you." Jackson let her go and pushed back so that he could look down at her. He looked a little shocked when he looked from me to Dru and back again. "Are you sure you guys are fraternal twins? The likeness is uncanny."

We'd gotten that question our entire lives. Yes, we were fraternal twins, although even though that was the case, I couldn't count all the times we'd been mistaken for each other over the years.

"And . . . I'm working on it," Jackson added with a grin, answering her initial question.

"Good," Dru managed, then pushed back and said, "Now, stop touching me."

"My sister's not a big hugger," I informed Jackson with a grin, then allowed myself to be enveloped into his arms and sighed happily. After a moment of goodness, I tilted my head back to look up at him and offer him my mouth for a *hello* kiss.

Jackson complied, and within seconds I was putty in his arms.

A chorus of, *"Get a room,"* was shouted by our group, so when Jackson released me, we were both laughing.

"Um, *hello*, aren't you going to introduce me, or is Dru the only sister that matters?"

"Sorry." I moved out of Jackson's arms to let Tasha step up. "Jackson, this is my sister, Tasha. Tasha, Jackson."

"It's great to finally meet you," Jackson said, and I could tell he was unsure whether or not he should hug her, since Dru hadn't been a fan, but he needn't have worried because Tasha threw her arms around his middle.

"Tash *is* a hugger," I said with a grin.

"I am," she said, pushing back and looking at him like I did, except her face was serious when she added, "But if you hurt my big sis, I'll cut you."

"Noted," Jackson chuckled. He let my sister go, then turned to the table and said, "My buddies, Ty and Rob, and Jan, Rob's wife. This is Tasha, and Dru, and, of course, Millie."

We walked around saying hi and introducing ourselves more intimately, as the waitress came up and took our drink orders. We had all just taken our seats around the table, with me sitting in between Jackson and Ty, with Dru and Tasha across from me, when a pretty blonde with a stylish outfit and nerves flitting on her face approached the table.

"Hey, sorry I'm late," she said quietly.

Ty and Rob looked surprised, but Jackson jumped up and said, "You're just on time, Rebecca," then he looked around the table before saying, "Ty, why don't you scoot down one and let Rebecca in."

"Ah, sure," Ty said, still seeming surprised, making me wonder what was going on.

Rebecca took the seat next to mine, and I could see her hand shaking slightly as she picked up the menu. Jackson made introductions again, and once he sat, I turned to Rebecca and said, "It's nice to meet you, Rebecca. So, you work with Jackson?"

Rebecca turned her head toward me and smiled briefly, then said, "Yes, I'm a teacher."

Ty leaned on the table to peer around Rebecca and shook his head.

"She's not just a teacher, she's the smartest teacher at the school. Teaches history while going for her doctorate in Education. Rebecca's brilliant."

Rebecca was still facing me, back to Ty, so I saw the pleasure suffuse her face and her breath catch at his words, and I understood . . . Rebecca had a crush, and my sweet guy was playing matchmaker.

I reached over to place my hand on Jackson's thigh and squeeze, then turned to kiss him lightly on the cheek.

He didn't know it yet, but he was totally getting lucky tonight.

We both were.

Jackson

Things were going great.

Millie's sisters seemed to like me, Ty and Rebecca were chatting each other up, and Rob's wife even gave in and let him eat the corned beef. We were all enjoying the drinks, atmosphere, and each other's company.

Then Jericho Smythe walked in.

I didn't notice at first. I was enjoying the feel of Millie pressed up against my side, her hand in mine as we laughed over Dru and Tasha's *worst clients ever* stories. I saw Ty shout a greeting and stand up out of the corner of my eye, but it wasn't until the three sisters stiffened and stopped talking that I looked up to see what was happening.

Jericho, normally self-assured and affable, was standing next to our table with his hands in his pockets and eyes wide as he took in our group.

"Glad you could make it," Ty was saying. "I know Sundays can be busy for you."

Jericho didn't hear him though, his eyes were frozen on Tasha, while she sat aghast, staring back at him.

Dru was rising, and from what little I knew about her, I figured she was about to tear my friend apart, and by the look on his face, I wasn't sure if he'd let her, or strike back. Wanting to keep the peace was part of my nature, and I really didn't want what had been a great night out to end with bloodshed or tears.

"Let's go grab you a drink," I said too loudly as I practically leapt out of my seat and grabbed Jericho by the bicep. "Another round?" I shouted over my shoulder, not bothering to wait for an answer.

I saw Dru and Millie gather around Tasha, while the rest of the table looked from them to Jericho and me in utter confusion.

"Are you okay?" I asked first. He was my friend, after all, and I didn't know what happened between him and Tasha, but it was obviously something painful for both of them.

Jericho looked to me, running his fingers through his hair as he leaned against the bar.

"Maker's neat," he told the bartender, then sighed and said, "Not really. I've done my best to avoid her . . . It was a shock, walking in and seeing her there."

"I'm sorry, man."

"Ty invited me, said you guys were getting together for a night out. I figured it'd be like the others, I didn't know . . ."

It wasn't unusual for Jericho to meet up with Ty, Rob, and me on one of our nights at the pub. This was the first time we invited anyone other than the group of us, so I could see why Jericho was blindsided. And, since the plan had only changed this week to include the women, Ty had probably invited him beforehand. Heck, he wouldn't have thought anything of Jericho being included with the women, since Jericho had never mentioned Tasha or any kind of past relationships to us before.

"Sorry, Ty didn't tell me, or I would have given you a head's up."

And I would have, to both Jericho and Millie.

"I don't know what to do," Jericho began as he took a healthy swig of whiskey. "If I leave, I look like a pussy, but . . . I don't know if I can be at the same table as her."

My eyebrows rose at that. Whatever had gone down between them must have been pretty bad, if they couldn't even stand to be in the same room.

I looked over my shoulder to see Millie hugging her sisters before they grabbed their things, said goodbye to my friends, then left the bar. Thankfully, Millie sat back down and smiled at something Jan was saying.

"Looks like you don't have to worry about it, Tasha and Dru left."

Jericho swung his head around, as if searching the bar to make sure they weren't hiding somewhere, then muttered, "*Fuck.*"

We went back to the table, with Jericho taking the seat that Dru had abandoned and me sliding next to Millie.

"I hope it's okay that I stayed," Millie whispered, her hand warming my forearm. "I told them you'd give me a ride home."

"Of course it is," I replied with a smile, dipping my head to run my nose slowly against the length of hers, before dropping a quick kiss on her lips. "I'm glad you stayed."

"They've been like this all night," I heard Rob joke.

I lifted my hand and gave him the finger, then tucked Millie as close to me as I could and looked at my friends' smiling faces. Well, everyone except Jericho, that is; he still looked like he'd been hit in the gut with a crowbar.

"I'm sorry, I didn't know you guys were going to be here. Your sisters didn't have to leave, I would have," Jericho told Millie.

"No, it's my fault," Ty put in, his face showing his regret. "I didn't know there was a history. It never occurred to me to tell you guys that Jericho was coming, or him that you were . . ."

"It's okay," Millie said softly, her face kind as she addressed not just Ty, but Jericho. "Tasha will be fine, she was just surprised. You guys should probably stop avoiding each other and hash things out, especially since not only do we own businesses across the street from each other, but now, we share friends."

Her hand found my thigh again as she spoke, and while her words warmed my heart, that hand was bringing something else to life.

"I know," Jericho said, his eyes dropping to the amber liquid in his glass.

"Great," Millie replied, then I almost jumped out of my seat again when her hand began to move upwards at a slow, torturous pace.

When she hit the top of my thigh and began to move closer to where my cock was getting harder by the second, I tried to school my features and keep my tone light as I said, "Whelp, it's been fun, but it looks like I need to get Millie home."

Millie

The ride home wasn't frenzied, with groping hands and heated looks. I thought it might be, after the way Jackson's body had reacted to my touch at the pub, but no. Instead, the cab of his truck was filled with anticipation.

It was like twenty minutes of foreplay, with barely any touching. Just the soft stroke of his thumb over the top of my hand, the rapid beat of my heart, and the occasional flash of his dimple when he clenched his teeth.

After we parked, I took Jackson's hand and led him up to my apartment. I didn't even spare a glance at my sisters' doors, even though I knew Tasha was upset about Jericho. I wanted to be there for her, I did, but she had Dru, and I'd go to her first thing in the morning.

Tonight, was about Jackson. *Me and Jackson.*

I closed the door behind us, locked it, and turned to him. My arms went around his neck as he lowered his face toward mine and brought his hands to clutch my waist, bringing me flush against him as our lips met.

He was hard, yet gentle, and the way his mouth worked mine had me moaning softly against his lips as I pressed my body closer to his.

I hadn't felt this in . . . *ever*. The rush of heat in my veins, the way my bones seemed to soften as my body became pliant and ready for him. The kiss was smooth and sweet, long and deep . . . It felt like we could stay that way forever, kissing in my entryway, but I wanted more.

My hand trailed down his arm, feeling the muscles bunched there, then moved lower until I reached his hand, pulled it from my waist, and captured it in mine. I broke away slowly, loving that look of desire on his face, the wetness on his lower lip, and the way his eyes were practically glazed over.

Smiling softly, knowingly, in what I really, *really* hoped was a sexy come-hither look, I guided him toward my bed.

I maneuvered him until he was sitting on the edge of bed in front of me, then I backed up a step, my eyes never leaving his. I was wearing a sleeveless button-up white blouse with a teal skirt that flirted above my knees, which swayed a bit with each movement. I pushed my long brown hair off of my shoulders, behind me, then started with the top button of my blouse, which was even with my cleavage, and began to free each button slowly.

Jackson's gaze was rapt on my fingers, his chest heaving with each breath he took.

I left my shirt hanging there for a moment, open but showing only a strip of skin, before slowly revealing my lace, see-through bra underneath as I pushed the shirt off and let it fall to the floor.

Then, bending at a torturing pace, I reached under my skirt and slid the matching lace boy shorts down my legs and stepped out of them.

"Come'ere," Jackson said gruffly.

So, I stepped in between his legs, until my breasts were even with his face. Jackson's hands hit the back of my thighs and slid up under my skirt until his fingertips hit the curve of my bottom.

We both groaned at the contact, and I became even louder when Jackson's lips sucked my hardened nipple through the lace in front of him, his hands caressing as he explored me. He moved to the other breast, and I widened my stance when he moved his exploration lower. Deeper.

"Jackson," I whispered, my head falling back as he teased my clit.

"Like velvet," I heard him say softly as he stroked the fire that had lit within me.

I was starting to float, getting swept up in the moment, as his finger entered me and my body began to rock in response. I reached around for the clasp of my bra and removed it quickly, then braced myself on his shoulders as another finger joined the first.

Finally, his hot, wet mouth was on my breasts with no interference. Licking, sucking, nipping across my sensitive flesh. The assault on my senses was almost too much; it had been too long, and never this good, and I was already fighting the need to come after just minutes of his ministrations.

My head fell forward as he worked me harder, and Jackson had to move his head back quickly before I hit his glasses.

"Sorry," I managed, a giggle bursting out of me as I thought of how horrible it would have been if I'd made contact. The giggle disappeared on a strangle as his thumb hit my clit and began rubbing circles as his fingers pumped in and out of me.

That took talent, I thought, right before I lost the ability to think.

I cried out as I came, Jackson milking every last bit out of me until I was ready to fall into a puddle at his feet. Before I could go completely boneless, Jackson urged my skirt down and lifted me, turning and laying me back on the bed.

I watched through my haze-filled eyes as he took off his clothes, enjoying each new expanse of skin as he unveiled them to me. He was tall, toned, and gorgeous, with a smattering of dark chest hair that V'd off as it trailed over his abs and beneath the boxer briefs he was currently taking off.

I knew I was smiling up at him like a drunken fool, even though I'd only had two drinks at the bar, my eyes tracking his every move as he rounded the bed, laid his glasses on my night table, and opened the condom he somehow had in his hand. I watched greedily as he smoothed it over his generous length, then climbed into bed.

Now next to me, no, Jackson moved until he was planking over me, his skin just a whisper above mine. And the sight of him there, above me, ready to claim me, become one with me, had my body waking from its languid slumber, eager to lose itself once again.

I opened my legs and brought my knees up as he settled there, his weight still on his forearms as I felt the hard, hot length of him against my core.

Jackson shifted his weight to one arm so he could bring his hand to my face, where he brushed my hair back from my forehead, then ran his fingertips over it. Caressing my cheekbone, the length of my nose, and my chin, before tracing my lips, as if he were memorizing the structure.

"Now a soft kiss—Aye, by that kiss, I vow an endless bliss," he said softly, before taking my lips and kissing me as if savoring every sip.

I sighed as I melted, his words affecting me just as much as his kiss, maybe more so.

When he broke the kiss, I whispered, "Who said that?"

"Keats," he replied, then moved to press his lips beneath my ear. Along my jaw. To the underside of my chin. Then, Jackson held my eyes as he slowly slid inside of me, neither of us breathing until he was fully seated and my legs wrapped around his waist.

"You feel amazing," Jackson managed, his breath labored as if he'd just ran five miles.

"So do you," I admitted, then smiled so widely at him I almost cried.

In that moment, I felt things I hadn't imagined I could.

I was falling for him so hard and so fast that the weight of it scared me, even as it thrilled me. His beautiful, kind face, with those dimples flashing, grinned back down at me, then he shifted and we both lost our smiles as we moaned at the delicious feeling of him inside of me.

With my legs around his waist, one hand in his hair and the other on his shoulder, Jackson began to move. Slowly at first, then faster, harder, until we were both lost, chasing our release, not knowing where he ended and I began.

It was the most beautiful experience of my life.

Jackson

I woke slowly, feeling more rested and sincerely happy than I'd felt in a really, *really* long time. Millie's bed was extremely comfortable, so much so that I was thinking of asking her what kind of mattress it was, and where she'd gotten the down comforter I was currently snuggled under.

Millie wasn't beside me, but I could still feel the warmth of her body, and smell the perfume of her hair as I stretched out across the most comfortable bed ever made.

Suddenly, I heard footsteps running toward me, before Millie landed right on top of me with a laugh and started pelting my face with kisses. I happily accepted the assault, then rolled smoothly until Mille was cradled half underneath me, and I was looking down at her gorgeous eyes, which were currently a deep green.

"Good morning to you, too," I murmured, then lowered my head to give her a deep, lingering kiss.

When I finally came up for air, Millie brushed her hand through my hair and said, "I made breakfast."

I immediately dropped her, jumped off the bed, and headed

toward the door, which made Millie burst into a fit of laughter that had me grinning back at her over my shoulder.

"What are you waiting for?" I joked as I watched her climb out of bed and walk toward me as I pulled on my boxer briefs.

She looked amazing. Long dark hair tussled after a night with my hands wrapped in it, her body encased beautifully in a knee-length floral nightgown that looked more like a dress than any pajamas I'd ever seen, but the real kicker was the look on her face. Or, more specifically, the way she was looking at me.

I could get used to a look like that . . .

"What'd you make?" I asked, my stomach grumbling at the thought of food.

"Crepes with berries and cream, scrambled eggs with ham and cheese, bacon, and biscuits," Millie replied.

I stopped and stared at her as she walked past me and into the kitchen.

"How long have you been awake?" I asked as I joined her.

She just chuckled and handed me a plate loaded with everything.

I took it, then grabbed one of the cups of coffee she had filled and took my winnings to the table. As soon as she sat down across from me and settled in, I picked up my fork and went to town.

It started with a whimper, then a moan, and by bite three, I was full on groaning.

"Just when I thought you were perfect and couldn't get any better," I began, absolutely meaning every word. "It's like you were made for me in a lab."

Millie blushed, then looked at me from under her eyelashes and admitted, "I said the same thing about you to my sisters when we met."

"Really?" I asked, extremely pleased by this new information.

When she nodded, her face flushed and sweet, I put down my fork and reached across the table for her hand. She gave it easily, and I leaned forward to bring it to my lips and kiss her lightly on the palm.

"I had an amazing time last night . . . No, that only scratches the surface . . . It was perfect, beautiful, right. Like it was meant to be," I said honestly. "I know it's kind of fast, but, Millie, I could fall for you so hard and fast, it's scary."

Millie's smile was wide, and her eyes grew misty as she replied, "I know, I feel the same way. It scares me a bit, even as it makes me extremely excited to find out what happens next."

"I don't want to ruin the mood, but I want you to know, I've filed the paperwork for my divorce and hired a PI to track down Julie. Once he does, she'll be served the papers, and that'll be that."

"That's . . . *great news*?" She looked unsure of whether she should be happy or sad that I was ending my marriage, and I understood that it was a complicated situation, but I needed her to know that it was what I wanted one hundred percent.

"It is great news," I assured her, then released her hand so we could both get back to breakfast. "You're not worried that I don't want the divorce, are you, because I assure you, it is."

Millie shook her head, then shrugged.

"I don't know . . . you've said that you want a divorce, that you'd never take her back, and I believe you, I do. *But*, you were married for a long time, you were each other's firsts for everything, and you have a child together. So, even though I believe you're telling truth, in the back of my head there's always a chance that you'll change your mind."

"I promise you, I won't. Even if I hadn't met you, and shared what we did last night . . . which, by the way, is *the* single most incredible night of my life. It's never been like that between Julie and I; in fact, I didn't know that was a thing. I'm afraid now that I know, you've created a monster, and I'm never going to let you out of my sight."

I could tell my words made her happy, but I could still see the twinge of doubt, and I knew the only thing that would erase that twinge would be to find Julie and finally put an end to this marriage.

"Well," I began, needing to get the subject off of my soon-to-be ex-wife for a while. "Now that we both know that we were made for each other, our chemistry is off the charts, and we both want to see where this is going, right?"

"Absolutely," Millie confirmed, allowing me to let go of that breath that had stuck in my throat when she brought up her doubts about me and Julie.

"I think it's time for you to meet Kayla." At her look of confusion, I knew I had to let her know what she was getting into. "I know you've already met, but that was before we were dating. I want us to do something together now that she knows we are, but I have to warn you, she's not all that *enthused* about our relationship."

Millie's face fell.

"She's not?"

"No," I admitted, my tone conveying my regret. "It's been just the two of us for a long time now, and like I said, I haven't seen anyone since Julie, so she's confused by the whole situation. She's still hurt by her mother leaving, and is holding on to the hope that Julie will come back and things will be the way they were. I know it won't be easy, but I think once she gets to spend some time with you, get to know you, and see how we are together, she'll come around."

"Okay," Millie agreed, although she looked doubtful.

Something occurred to me, and I figured since we were talking heavy, we might as well get it all out at once.

"Do you like kids? Want them? I just realized we never talked about it."

"Oh, yes," Millie said, her face clearing, and she brought her hand to grasp mine this time. "I love kids, and I want to have kids."

"Yeah? How many?"

"I've always thought three, because of how close my sisters and I are, although we weren't always close growing up, but I'm open to suggestions."

"And, marriage? Do you want to be married one day?"

"Yes, I want it all. A family, our business, the American dream," Millie said, squeezing my hand, a small smile playing on her lips. "Now that we've agreed to hire full-time help and start having lives outside of Three Sisters, it'll be easier for me to focus more on the personal part of my life. More on us."

"I can't wait," I admitted, and it was the truth.

I couldn't wait to see where this thing between Millie and me would lead.

Millie

"Okay, there's an important topic you've been avoiding, and we need to get serious. We're running out of time," Dru was saying from my chaise, where she was currently snuggled up with a glass of wine. "Our birthday party."

"Ugh," I groaned, throwing my head back and grunting as I hit the cushion behind me. "We're going to be twenty-nine, not nine, Dru. Aren't we getting a little old for parties?" I asked. "It's not even a milestone."

"Every birthday is a milestone," Dru said dryly, then looked to where our sister was laying on the floor and added, "Tasha's got my back on this one."

"I don't know," Tasha replied, tilting her head back so she was looking at us upside down. "Maybe Millie's right and we're getting too old to make such a fuss."

"*Too old*?" Dru asked with mock fury, sitting up so abruptly that she almost spilled red wine on my gray sofa. Luckily, she didn't. "We're still in our twenties, for crying out loud. We should be hitting the clubs, going nuts, instead we work our butts off and a night in with a bottle of wine is considered living it up. Come on, you guys, don't take my birthday away from me."

I couldn't help but laugh at my twin's dramatics, she'd always been more into parties and celebrations than me.

"What if this year, we only celebrate your birthday with a party, the way you want to?" I suggested. "Mine can be more low key, the way I want it."

Dru looked at me as if I'd grown another head in the last few minutes.

"We share the same birthday, Millie," she said, telling me something I obviously already knew. "We've *always* celebrated together."

"That's my point. Wouldn't you rather have a party focused solely on you, instead of on both of us?"

She narrowed her eyes on me and asked, "Do you already have something planned with Jackson, is that why you're trying to separate things?"

"No, I haven't even told him our birthday is coming up yet."

"You totally need to tell him. If he recited Keats to you while *making love*, I bet he'd do up your birthday all kinds of romantic," Tasha said on a sigh.

I'd regretted telling them about Jackson's words almost as soon as they were out of my mouth, but I'd been floating on a cloud and it had just spilled out.

"Shut it," I ordered as I threw a pillow at Tasha's head, which she avoided with a giggle.

"Are you serious about this?" Dru asked, still hung up on the birthday thing. Seriously, the girl *loved* parties, especially in her honor, and I'd never really cared one way or another. Maybe it was time for us to start doing things separately. Our lives had always been practically interchangeable, and although it was scary, I knew they couldn't remain that way forever.

"Yes," I replied, smiling at my sister. "Do it up however you want. Whatever theme, whatever food, anything you want."

"But, what about you?" she asked softly.

"We can go out to lunch or something . . . Oh, I know, we can do brunch. With champagne. And, I'll come to your party."

"You don't think that would be weird?"

"What do you say we give it a try this year, and see how it goes, then, next year, we'll have a big blowout for our thirtieth?" I suggested.

"I'll hold you to that," Dru warned.

"I know," I said with a laugh.

"Deal," Dru said, then looked between me and Tasha and added, "So, we have one week to plan the best Speakeasy-themed party ever!"

"I think I know a catering company that can pull it off," Tasha joked.

"I don't know, it's kind of short notice," I argued.

"Good thing I blocked the date on the calendar six months ago," Dru countered.

"Of course you did," I laughed.

Tasha pushed herself up and off of the floor, crossed to get the open bottle of wine, then proceeded to refill our glasses.

"I'm sorry I didn't get a chance to stop by and see how you were doing last night," I began, watching my younger sister closely for any signs of duress. "How are you doing now, with the whole Jericho thing?"

Tasha tossed the empty bottle in the trash, then came back to sit cross-legged on the floor in front of us. She'd always been the kind of person who'd rather sit on the floor than on furniture; weird, I know, but that was our Tasha.

"I was totally taken off-guard, you know? We were having a good time, watching Ty and Rebecca make a love connection, while laughing at Rob trying to hide beer from Jan, who obviously knew what he was doing, then . . . Bam! Jericho." Her eyes widened and she took a big gulp of her wine. "It's crazy that they're all friends, isn't it? Totally unexpected."

"Yeah, I'm so sorry, I had no idea that it was even a possibility that he'd be there," I assured her. "I mean, Jackson said they were, like, sports-watching friends, but I didn't know Jericho was actually a friend he hung out with a lot."

"It's not your fault, and I'm so sorry that I left like that. Jackson must think I'm a drama queen."

Tasha laid back, resting her wine glass on her chest. I moved off the couch to sit next to her on the floor.

"No, he doesn't think that, he likes you both. I think he felt bad, they all did. No one wanted you to feel like you had to leave."

"I know," Tasha said softly, her eyes coming to mine as she admitted, "He looked really, *really* good. Even better than he used to."

"I'm sorry, babe, and I know you don't want to hear this, but you should talk to him. Hash it all out and get closure once and for all."

"Yeah," she replied, but neither the look on her face nor her tone made it seem like she would be eager to do that any time soon.

Jackson

The week had, thankfully, gone by quickly. It was a usual week filled with lesson plans, homework, and Kayla, so I'd had plenty to do, but now I had the added bonus of yearning for Millie.

Yeah, I said it, and I'm man enough to admit it. I yearned for her.

The night we'd spent together was always at the forefront of my mind, distracting me at the most inopportune moments. Flashes of her lips curled up, the feel of her soft skin, the little noises she'd made when I was inside of her, hit me when I was standing in the checkout line of the grocery store, making dinner for Kayla and me, or, most often, when I was reading aloud to my students.

Once again, we'd mostly been communicating between texts and phone calls, which was great, but, *man*, I missed the feel of her in my arms. We needed to move forward with her spending time with Kayla, so that *I* could get more time with her.

Which was why I was currently making tacos, rice, beans, and salsa, even though it wasn't Tuesday. It was Kayla's favorite meal, and Millie was taking a dinner break to join us for about an hour to get to know Kayla better.

Humming to myself, I cut up the vegetables to top the tacos and kept glancing at the clock. The anticipation was killing me, but I couldn't keep the smile off my face.

"Do I smell tacos?" I heard Kayla asked from behind me and turned to see her sniffing at the air as she walked into the kitchen. "But, it's Thursday."

"You do, and we're starting a new craze, *Taco Thursday,*" I joked, my stomach clenching nervously as my little girl's eyes narrowed on me.

I shouldn't be afraid of re-introducing my daughter to my girlfriend, at least, *I hope she's my girlfriend*, but I was. After her initial reaction to Millie, I knew this wasn't going to be an easy thing for her to accept, and although I wanted the evening to go smoothly, I had a feeling I was in for some bumps.

Rather than reply, Kayla just stood there, arms crossed, staring at me as she waited for me to come clean about what was really going on.

Seriously, her teenaged years are going to be terrifying . . .

"I thought it would be fun if Millie came by for dinner so you guys could get to know each other."

As soon as Millie's name left my lips, Kayla scowled.

"Now," I kept going as if I hadn't noticed the death glare. "She only has an hour break before she has to get back to work, so remember your manners, and be the sweet, thoughtful girl I've raised you to be."

Rather than respond as I'd hoped, her lower lipped popped out. Before I could think of any other way to bribe her into being on her best behavior, the doorbell rang.

My immediate reaction was to grin and run to the door. I held back from running, but couldn't hold back the grin. I looked at Kayla on my way to the door, and saw that the scowl was gone and she was watching me with a mixture of fear, hurt, and panic.

Shit, throwing a fit was one thing, but I didn't want my little girl hurting over my decisions.

"Come here," I said, stopping to crouch in front of her. I pulled her into my arms and hugged her close, and even though she didn't return the gesture, I promised, "You'll always be my number one girl."

Pulling back, I kissed her on the forehead, before standing up and rushing to let Millie in.

"Hey, sorry." I opened the door and gave her a quick kiss on the cheek, wishing it was more, but knowing Kayla would freak if I had a full-on make-out session on the porch. "Come on in."

"It's okay, I haven't been here long," Millie assured me with a sweet smile, her eyes taking in my face as if she hadn't seen me in weeks.

It felt good to know that she'd missed me as much as I'd missed her.

I stepped aside to let her walk passed, then gestured at Kayla, who was still standing by the kitchen where I'd left her. She didn't look exactly welcoming, but at least she wasn't shooting Millie her death glare.

"Kayla, you remember Millie, who gave you the tea party that you loved so much," I tried, but Kayla didn't take the bait.

"Hi, Kayla, it's great to see you again," Millie said with a little too much enthusiasm when Kayla didn't say anything. "Thanks for letting me join you for dinner."

"It's just tacos," Kayla said with a shrug, causing me to shoot her a glare of my own, which I hoped conveyed that she'd be grounded if she kept this up.

"Well, I love tacos," Millie said happily, as if Kayla wasn't being a brat. "I think they should be made into a new food group, all their own."

"Millie would know, she's a chef," I said, noticing for the first time that Millie was still in her chef coat, which was intimidating, since *I* was cooking for *her*. "Just so you know, these are just regular old ground beef tacos, nothing too fancy."

Millie laughed and began unbuttoning her chef coat, which snagged my attention and made me thing of the last time she'd undressed in front of me.

No, bad brain, think of tacos, football, a hairy naked man riding bareback . . .

"Your tacos are the best, Daddy," Kayla said, joining us as she came to my defense.

"Thanks, baby," I replied, dropping a kiss on her head as I tried to avoid Millie *finally* unbuttoning the last button.

"Don't want to make a mess on this," Millie said as she shrugged out of the coat and laid it over the back of the couch. I did *not* notice how fantastic she looked in her tank top with little pink roses as she turned to Kayla and added, "I'm sure his tacos are wonderful. I can't wait to try them."

"I know you're on a schedule, so let's go ahead and eat," I suggested, holding my arms out so that both Kayla and Millie could walk in front of me.

As I followed, I prayed that the next hour wouldn't get my daughter grounded, or ruin my budding relationship.

Millie

I knew I shouldn't be so nervous; she was a nine-year-old girl. I'd once been a nine-year-old girl, so I knew what it felt like. Still, Kayla had made it no secret that she would rather be eating glass than sitting down to a meal with me, and Jackson was trying so hard to pretend that everything was going well, that he was giving my nerves hives.

"Millie and her sisters started their business all on their own and are now so successful that they're expanding. Isn't that great? Just goes to show you, that if you find something that you love, and put your heart into it, you can make your dreams come true."

I caught Kayla's eye roll at Jacksons attempt at a life lesson, but luckily, he hadn't. I think that would have been the final straw that made him blow a gasket.

My face was beginning to hurt from holding the smile that I'd had plastered on my face since dinner began, but I powered through and maintained my pleasant expression.

"Oh, Jackson, I know I mentioned Dru's Speakeasy birthday party to you, but Dru wanted me to have you invite Rob, Jan, Ty, and

Rebecca as well," I told him when the thought popped in my head.

"Oh, okay, sure, I'll pass it along," he replied, his tone conveying his stress over this not-so-enjoyable dinner. Then he blinked twice and put his taco down. "Wait, if it's Dru's birthday, then it's yours, too. Aren't you having a party with her?"

I shook my head and explained, "We've always done one together, but I'm more low-key than Dru, and I wanted to give her the chance to go nuts and have the party she's always wanted. It'll be weird, but it's not like we won't still be together all day, and celebrate together, but I wanted her to have something fun for herself. We will be having a lunch that day to celebrate my birthday, and I'd love it if you could come. *Both* of you."

"This Sunday?" Jackson asked.

When I nodded, Kayla shoved the rest of her taco in her mouth, then said, "Iawayamd bsjia."

"Kayla," Jackson warned, but she ignored him and started talking with her mouth full again.

That's when he snapped.

Jackson's cup landed on the table with a clatter and his chair flew back as he stood.

"Go to your room, *now*. We'll discuss your punishment after I calm down."

Kayla looked startled, then her eyes filled before she shot a glare at me, rose from the table, and stomped off.

I held my breath until her door slammed and Jackson sat back down with a sigh, pushing his glasses up his nose as he looked at me apologetically.

"I'm so sorry," he began. "She's a sweet girl, I swear it. I know that's probably hard for you to believe after the way she just acted. I'm not sure what's gotten into her, but I'll talk to her."

"It wasn't so bad," I lied, hoping to make him feel better.

"How could it have been worse?" he asked incredulously.

"She could have stabbed me with her fork," I joked, and felt some of the tension ease when he grinned.

"Well, thank God for small favors."

"I have to get going soon, but let me help you with this," I said, standing so I could start clearing the table.

"Don't worry about that," Jackson countered, then snagged my hand and gave it a tug. "Come here."

With a quick glance to where Kayla had disappeared, I allowed him to pull me into his lap, putting my arms around his shoulders as I sat.

"I missed you," Jackson admitted sweetly, causing me to smile down at him.

His glasses were a little askew, so I fixed them, my stomach clenching when his dimples popped out at the gesture.

"I missed you, too," I returned softly, watching his eyes as I lowered my face slowly toward him.

Our lips brushed gently once, then twice, before his hand on my back applied more pressure, urging me closer, and his lips parted beneath mine. The kiss was delicate and full of yearning, and I wished desperately that I didn't have to leave him and go back to work. It seemed like *ages* since I'd been in his arms, and I was eager to lose myself in him again.

As soon as possible.

"So, Sunday?" I asked when we broke apart. I rested my forehead against his and tried not to count the hours until I'd see him again. Why did Sunday suddenly feel so far away?

"Yes, for lunch, and the party. I'll talk to the guys and let you know if they can make it, so you can pass it along to Dru."

"Sounds perfect."

"Text me tonight when you get off work?" Jackson asked, his voice full of the same longing that was in my heart.

"I will," I promised.

Reluctantly I stood and asked, "Are you sure you don't want help?" Indicating the mess from dinner.

"I've got it."

I nodded, and with no other reason to stay, I knew I had to get back in order to not get behind. Once I had my chef coat back on, Jackson walked me to the door and gave me one last kiss.

"Thanks for coming," he said, and when he opened his mouth to apologize once more for Kayla, I put a finger against his lips to stop his words.

"Thanks for inviting me," I whispered, then tilted my head and added, "Don't worry, she'll come around."

I was walking back to my car when I felt eyes on me, so I looked over my shoulder to find Kayla watching me from her window. I lifted my hand and waved goodbye, but was disheartened when she quickly closed her pink and purple-striped curtains and disappeared.

As I got in my car and drove back to work, I hoped I wasn't wrong about Kayla warming up to me.

Jackson

By the time I got to the restaurant, I was practically skipping. It was Millie's birthday, the first major event that we were celebrating together, and I may be hiding the *best gift ever* in my back pocket.

I'd never been that great at gift giving. Julie never really collected anything, or made a big deal about presents. It wasn't until Kayla got old enough to start unwrapping gifts and began to light up over every little thing that I became the gift-giving guru.

And, I'd really outdone myself this time . . .

I'd enlisted Dru and Tasha's help, and based off of their feedback, Millie's mind was about to be blown.

I grinned as I approached the table at the Thai restaurant that Millie had chosen, and was pleased to note that she'd left the chair next to her open for me. I bent to kiss her softly on the forehead before taking my seat and saying hi to Dru and Tasha.

"Sorry for being a few minutes late. I was waylaid dropping of Kayla."

After her reaction to being invited to Millie's lunch, and

subsequent grounding for rude behavior, I'd decided it would be best for everyone if I took Kayla to my parents' instead.

"You're not late, we haven't even ordered yet," Millie assured me, and I couldn't help but reach under the table and take her hand.

The need to touch her at all times was almost overwhelming.

"Great," I said as I picked up my menu. I'd never been to this place before and had no idea what I was going to order. "You all ready for tonight?"

"Yes, our minions are finishing up the decorations now. I cannot wait to see it," Dru gushed, obviously excited. Then looked to her sister and said, "But, that's for later, we're here to focus on Millie now. So, come on, birthday girl, tell us the best part of the last year and what you most hope to accomplish in the coming year."

Millie looked to me and explained, "It's a tradition for us. Mom started it when we were still in middle school. She always believed that you wouldn't achieve success without goals, so she always wanted us to have them."

"She sounds amazing."

"She was," Millie said, sadness crossing her features. "I wish you could have met her, she would like you."

"Me too," I replied, then, hoping to bring her happiness back, I asked, "So, what was the best part of your year? Other than meeting me, of course."

I was happy when she blushed prettily at my joke, and said, "Of course. Um . . . I guess I'd have to say not only the success of Three Sisters, but that we're doing well enough to grow our full-time employees and ease up on our hours a bit. In the next year, I'd like to see more of that. On the flip side, I'd also like us to start doing more of the upscale children's party, like we discussed." She squeezed my hand and smiled. "That idea came from you, and

Kayla's tea party."

"Glad we could help." I grinned, thinking how lucky it was that she'd agreed to help me that day.

"Can I get your drink orders?" the server said from next to me, causing me to jump in my seat, since I hadn't heard him approach.

"Thai Tea, please," Millie said.

"Make that three," Tasha revised.

I looked at the three of them, then up at the waiter and asked, "What's Thai Tea?"

"You've never had it?" Dru asked.

"Oh, you have to order it," Tasha added.

"It's really good," Millie concurred.

"Guess you can make that four, then," I told the waiter, who nodded and took off to get our drinks.

"Soooo, another one of our traditions is to get up earlier and do presents in bed," Tasha started.

"Which means, Millie and I already opened our presents from each other," Dru added.

"*Guys*," Millie chastised, when she realized they were fishing to see if I'd gotten her something.

Although, they weren't fishing, they knew darn well what I'd gotten her.

My face split with a grin, and I clapped my hands together in excitement, "Well . . ." But before I could do the big reveal, my phone started ringing.

"Sorry, I'd better take this, just in case it's about Kayla," I apologized as I rose from my chair.

"Of course," Millie said sweetly.

I took a few steps toward the side of the room, then stopped in my tracks when I saw it was Mick calling. Figuring I might need more privacy, I walked toward the exit as I pressed the button to answer the phone and held it to my ear.

"Hello?"

"Heeler? It's Mick. Thought you'd like to know I found her," he replied briskly.

"Julie?" I asked dumbly, even though that was the only person he could be talking about.

"Yeah."

"Where?" I asked, looking out over the street without actually seeing anything.

"She's in Hampton, about forty minutes away."

"*Forty minutes*?" I whispered with disbelief. "She's been forty minutes away from our daughter this *entire* time and has *never once* tried to see her?"

"Sorry, bro, she's a piece . . . Living with some rich old dude in a fancy house. Cheats on him with her tennis instructor *and* the pool guy."

"*What*?" I asked, then had to clarify. "You are talking about Julie, right? Julie Heeler?"

"The one and only. 'Cept she goes by Julie Baker now."

Her maiden name. She'd reverted back to her maiden name and was living forty minutes away from our daughter, without so much as a *god-damned Happy Birthday* . . .

"What's the address?" I asked. "I've gotta swing by and get the divorce papers, then I'm heading over there. I need to get this done once and for all."

Mick gave me the address and clipped, "I'll meet you there."

Then he hung up and I stood there, staring at nothing and wondering how Mick could be talking about the woman I'd been married to and had a beautiful child with, because the person he'd just described was an absolute stranger.

Millie

"Are you ready to order?"

I looked up to see the waiter standing patiently next to me. Our drinks were in front of us, and it had been five minutes since Jackson had left to take his call. I looked toward the door he'd exited, hoping to see him walking back in, but he didn't.

"Just a few more minutes, please," I replied, then looked at my sisters and said, "I'm going to go check on Jackson."

When I opened the door and stepped outside, I saw him standing on the curb staring off into space, his phone in his hand by his side.

"Hey," I began, causing Jackson to flinch and turn his head toward my voice. "Is everything okay with Kayla?"

"Uh . . . yeah," he replied, running his empty hand through his hair and letting out a deep sigh before turning fully toward me. Jackson lifted his hand holding his phone and said, "That was Mick, my PI."

"Oh." I looked down at the phone, which now only showed a blank screen, and asked, "Did he find her?"

Jackson's face was pained when he replied, "Yes."

Not sure what to say, I waited, hoping he'd let me know what was bothering him, and honestly a little nervous about what his reaction to finding his wife was going to be. Would he want to go back to her after all, now that he knew where she was? Was he hoping for a reconciliation, if not for his sake, then for Kayla's?

I know Jackson meant it when he said he didn't want her back, but will that change when he actually sees her again?

"Julie's in Hampton. *Hampton*. Do you know where that is?" Jackson asked, his voice rising.

I nodded, because I did know where it was, and it wasn't that far away.

He took a deep breath. "I have to go see her. Talk to her . . . My lawyer has the papers drawn up, he said that he can give them to me right away, or serve them himself. But, I think I have to do it . . . ya know?"

"I do." And, I did. I knew he needed answers, because without them, he may never get closure, for himself and for Kayla.

If closure is what they want . . .

"You should go," I told him, even though it made me sick to say it.

"But," Jackson began, looking miserable as he looked over my head at the restaurant behind him.

"It's okay," I assured him.

"Millie, it's your birthday lunch, I'm not just gonna . . ."

Putting my hands on his shoulders, I looked up into his sweet handsome face, taking in his disheveled hair, glasses, and the telltale lack of dimples.

"You need to go handle this; it's time. It'll still be my birthday later, and I'll see you at Dru's party."

"Are you sure?" Jackson asked, obviously torn.

"Positive," I said with a nod.

"Okay, but I *will* see you later, and we'll celebrate your birthday after Dru's party, just the two of us." Jackson frowned, then leaned down to press his forehead against mine. "I really hate to do this to you on your birthday, but I have to see her, face to face, and now that I know where she is, I feel like I wouldn't be able to concentrate on anything else until I did, and that wouldn't be fair to you either."

"I understand."

"You're amazing," he whispered, pulling back to look down at me as he smoothed my hair back in a sweet gesture. "I'll save your present until tonight. I don't want it to be tainted by this."

"Okay," I agreed with a somewhat forced smile. "I look forward to it."

I stepped back, and could see Jackson still warring with indecision, so I pointed down the street and ordered, "Go, and I'll see you tonight."

Jackson nodded, then walked away. I stood there watching, smiling for real when he looked back over his shoulder, then blew me a kiss.

After a couple seconds, I went back in to the restaurant and sat at the table.

"What's going on?" Dru asked, looking over my shoulder for Jackson, then frowning when she realized he wasn't with me.

"His PI found his wife. He's going to go see her and give her the divorce papers."

"Now?" Tasha cried. "Couldn't it have waited until after lunch?"

"He left your birthday lunch?" Dru asked incredulously.

"You guys, I told him to go. He would have been thinking about confronting her, and I'd be worrying about how he was doing and everything. It's just better that he goes and handles everything now.

Get it over with. I'll see him at the party tonight, and he said we'll celebrate my birthday after."

"Are you sure you're okay?" Dru asked, her hand reaching for mine.

I grasped it gratefully and admitted, "I'm happy he's found her, and hopeful that he'll get the answers and closure that he needs . . ."

"But, you're worried," my twin guessed.

"What if they see each other and realize they should still be a family?" I asked softly.

"Then you'll get through it, with us by your side. Together, we can do anything, right?"

"Right," Tasha confirmed.

"Would you like to order now?" our waiter asked.

"Yes," I confirmed. "It'll just be the three of us. Can you get me the Butter Chicken, and change this Thai Tea for dirty martini, extra dirty, with three olives?"

"Yas!" Dru exclaimed, clapping her hands together. "Make that three martinis' and I'll have the curry."

"Me too," Tasha said, and we all handed the waiter our menus.

Inadvertently, my eyes drifted back toward the door, then I felt Dru squeeze my hand and Tasha grab my other one, and I turned my attention to my sisters.

"It'll be okay," Dru assured me, and I prayed she was right.

Jackson

My heart was pounding, stomach cramping, and I felt a little light-headed as I followed the GPS to where Julie had been hiding for the past year.

As I eased up to the curb, I noticed Mick getting out of a beat-up old Army Jeep. As his large body lumbered toward me, my gaze kept darting to the large house to the right of us. There was nothing homey or cozy about it; no, it was nothing like the home we'd build together. This one was flashy. *Ostentatious*.

"She's in there," Mick assured me as he approached. "I saw her come back about twenty minutes ago and she hasn't reemerged."

I nodded, unable to find my voice quite yet.

"I'll wait out here, unless you need me to come with you," Mick stated, his eyebrow raised. I wasn't sure if that eyebrow was him daring me not to be a wuss, or him simply waiting for my reply, but I took a deep breath and dug deep.

"No, I've got it," I replied, clutching the manila folder that held my key to freedom.

Mick leaned against the side of my truck as I rounded it and walked slowly up the sidewalk, as if I were walking *The Green Mile*. I felt an adrenaline rush at the thought of finally having this confrontation, months and months of questions and a myriad of feelings swimming through me, as I approached the door and knocked.

Nothing . . .

I rang the doorbell and waited.

Nothing . . .

"Are you sure she's still here?" I shouted back at Mick, who gave me a look like I should know better than to question him.

A second later, I heard noise from the other end of the door, and was adjusting my glasses nervously on my nose when it opened. My breath caught, but it took me a full three count to realize that the woman standing in front of me *was*, in fact, Julie.

Everything about her was different.

She was wearing a string bikini, which showed off the fact that she'd had her breasts enlarged and that she was tiny, like really, really tiny. I could probably wrap my arms around her waist if I wanted to, which I didn't. Her naturally dark hair had been bleached to almost a white blonde, and her nose looked different. Not a drastic change, but enough that *I* knew she'd had work done.

Her skin was dark, tanned, which highlighted the stretch marks that had developed when she was pregnant with Kayla. Those marks, along with her eyes, were the only evidence that this was the Julie that I'd been married to.

"*Jackson*?" Julie breathed out, her smile faltering. "What are you doing here? How'd you find me?"

I looked over my shoulder at Mick, and Julie leaned to the side to see around me, then righted herself as I struggled to make the words come out of my mouth. To say I was shocked, flabbergasted, *reeling*, would be an understatement.

"Well, at first I thought you'd come back," I began, my voice scratchy as if I'd just woken from a long slumber. "Then I worried you'd been hurt. Eventually, I just stopped caring." Her flinch told me that I'd hit my target, but even though I'd wanted to inflict pain on her, just as she had on me, I realized that this wasn't why I was there, and it didn't make me feel any better to hurt her. "Once I hired him," I gestured over my shoulder at Mick with my thumb, "it wasn't that hard. You've been here the whole time?"

"Why don't you come inside," Julie offered, stepping back a bit and gesturing behind her.

"I don't want to," I said, a little more forcefully than necessary. "I just came here for some answers, and to give you this." I held the envelope up in between us, then dropped my hand again.

"What's that?" she asked, but I shook my head and said, "Answers first."

Julie sighed, as if I were the one being unreasonable, then stated, "I already told you when I left, I needed time to find myself. To *be* me."

"But you never said why, or how you weren't already being you . . . I don't understand, and Kayla surely doesn't. Do you remember her, your daughter? She just turned nine, did you even remember it was her birthday?"

My emotions were getting the better of me, and I couldn't stop, even though I saw her flinch again at my rant.

"How was I holding you back? How was being a mother? I don't get it? I never denied you anything, or told you no when you wanted to do something. Our relationship wasn't like that, at least I didn't think so. I thought we were partners, that we shared everything and used each other for support when we needed it. You totally blindsided me, Julie. One second I thought everything was fine, and the next, you were gone. What happened?"

I realized I needed to actually breathe and pause, to let her respond, and I needed to gain control before I embarrassed myself by crying in front of her. Or, God forbid, in front of Mick. Heaving with emotion, I watched her face. She crinkled her nose up, just like she always did when she was nervous, then shifted her weight from her left foot to her right.

"I read this book, then watched a YouTube video, about settling. About becoming something you want for the sake of others, and I realized that I'd never gotten to live the life that I'd always dreamed of as a kid. I never sowed my oats, or went wild, or just, you know, lived. We never meant to get pregnant and married like that, neither of us did, but we did what we had to and you seemed to thrive, Jackson. It was obvious you loved being a father and a husband, and your job . . . you really enjoyed teaching. You were happy. And the happier you were, the more I began to resent you."

"Why?" I asked, the question coming out strangled.

"Because I wasn't happy. I loved you and Kayla, I did, I swear, but it felt like you were sucking the life out of me. And the more time that passed, the less of me there was. Reading that book was like waking up after sleeping for ten years. We only get one life, and it's pretty short, and I knew if I didn't leave, and go figure out what I wanted, who I wanted to be, I'd be lost."

"Why didn't you tell me that you felt that way? I would have helped you try and figure things out. I never wanted you to be unhappy," I asked imploringly, because she was right, I had been happy and I'd had no idea that my wife wasn't.

"I don't know, I just couldn't. I'm sorry that I left like that, sorry that I hurt you, but I've found what I was looking for, Jackson. I am happy." Julie attempted a smile, shifted again, and I knew she was as ready to be done with the conversation as I was, but I still had to ask . . .

"And, Kayla? What about our daughter? Don't you miss her? Want to see her?" I'd already come to terms with things being over between the two of us, but I couldn't understand her not needing to see Kayla.

Julie bit her lip and looked away.

"I think it's better this way . . ."

"Better for her to grow up without her mother?" I pushed, my tone conveying my disbelief, my anger.

"I don't have anything to offer her right now, maybe some day . . ."

Holding up my hand again, I shoved the manila envelope at her.

"These are divorce papers. I'm asking for full custody, the house, everything . . . everything you left behind. If you want to fight me for Kayla, I'll fight, but if you want half of the house or anything in it, we can sit down and draw up new papers."

I was done. Angry, heartbroken for my daughter, and eager to get back to Millie, her sisters, and my friends. I needed a strong drink, the arms of the woman I was falling for, and tomorrow, I would hug my daughter until she had no doubt in her mind that I loved her enough for two parents.

"I don't want anything," Julie said, taking the papers from my hand.

"There's a pen in there, and a yellow tab next to everywhere you need to initial and sign."

She nodded and began doing just that.

"You should call your parents, they miss you terribly," I informed her as I watched her sign.

Julie looked up at that, her eyes flashing.

"How are they?"

"Not good. Your mom's getting thinner and she's always sad. Your dad spends a lot of time tinkering in his garage. They're both hurting. You need to call them, Julie."

She let out a breath and said, "I will."

I took the papers she offered and flipped through them, making sure everything was signed and initialed according to my lawyer's instructions. When I was satisfied they were, I put everything back in the envelope and looked at my soon-to-be ex-wife one last time.

"If you wake up and realize what your missing, give me a call and we can figure out how to reintroduce you into Kayla's life. You do not try to go around me and contact her yourself. I need to be involved and we need to do what we can to make things comfortable for her."

Julie nodded, but didn't respond, so I said, "Goodbye, Julie," and turned to go back to my truck.

"Jackson," she called, and I turned in the middle of the sidewalk to look back at the stranger who used to be my wife. "I'm sorry."

Without a word, I turned back to my truck, told Mick I'd follow him back to his office, then left Hampton, and Julie, behind.

Millie

My flapper dress was purple with lots of fringe, which swayed any time I made a move. I absolutely loved it, along with the amazing decorations our team had come up with.

The banquet room had been converted into a speakeasy, compete with whiskey barrels as tables, a mugshot photo station, prohibition signs everywhere, and you even had to use the secret code word to get in.

Dru, in a dress identical to mine, only black, was already having the time of her life, and we'd only been here for about thirty minutes. Louis Armstrong was playing in the background and everyone was eating, drinking, and laughing. Having a great time.

But I couldn't stop watching the door, and checking my phone. I was worried about Jackson, wondering if he'd spoken to Julie and how that had gone.

"Everything okay?"

Tasha came up next to me, a drink in each hand, and passed one to me.

She looked adorably sexy in a black pinstripe suit with nothing but a camisole underneath, her bright-red hair styled perfectly for the era in finger waves, her lips a bright red.

"Thanks," I said, accepting the glass. "And, yes, I'm fine."

"Haven't heard from him yet?" she guessed.

"No, not yet."

"Don't worry, he'll show," Tasha assured me, her voice full of more confidence than I was feeling.

"I know," I lied.

Commotion toward the entrance had me looking over to see a motley crew walking in. Ty, Rebecca, Rob, and Jan, all decked out and looking dapper in their twenties costumes. My breath caught as I looked behind them, hoping to see Jackson, and there he was, except he wasn't wearing a twenties costume.

No, he was showing off a lot of skin in his tiny white board shorts, Hawaiian shirt, which was, no lie, tied at his waist, with a captain hat on his head.

Jackson's eyes caught mine and he grinned, then did his best saunter all the way to me. By the time he reached me, I was laughing so hard that I was practically bent over. When he stopped in front of me and attempted to gyrate, I clapped a hand over my mouth as I guffawed.

His eyes were twinkling as he watched me, and when I finally had some control, I uncovered my mouth and said, "That's some Elvis costume."

"Thank you, *thank you very much*," was Jackson's reply, which had Tasha groaning next to me.

"Oh my God!"

"I know, right, it's awful," Ty said, giving his friend a onceover and grimacing.

"I love it," I purred as I put my arms around his waist and tilted my head back to look at him. "You look amazing."

"Don't encourage him." This came from Rob, as he picked up a cigar off of the table next to him and ran it under his nose. When Jan snatched it out of his hand he said, "*Hey . . .*"

Jan just gave him a look, and he closed his mouth and pouted, causing the rest of us to laugh.

"How are you?" I asked softly, while everyone else teased Rob.

"Never been better," Jackson said with a huge grin. "It's over."

I leaned in to hug him tightly, then looked back up at him and asked, "And Kayla?"

Jackson shook his head sadly, then his face cleared and he asked, "Can you step out for a minute? I want to give you your present."

"Now?" I asked, looking around at the party in full swing. "Don't you want to wait until we get home?"

Jackson picked me up, causing me to laugh as he answered excitedly, "I can't wait that long."

"Okay," I said as he put me down, then took my hand in his and led me toward the door at the back of the room, which led out to a balcony.

The party was muted when he slid the sliding glass door shut behind us and we stepped out into the night.

"Wow," I said as I looked up at the stars glittering in the sky. "What a beautiful night."

"Only more so because you're in it," Jackson replied, pulling me in close to his side, and my heart melted.

I leaned my head against his shoulder, enjoying the moment, a happy sigh emitting from my lips, when he nudged me and asked, "Don't you want your present?"

"Oh yeah, that's why we came out here," I said with mock

surprise, then put my hands out in front of me and closed my eyes. "What is it? Gimme?"

Jackson chuckled at my exuberance, then laid what felt like paper in my hand. I opened one eye and peeked at him, saw his excited face, and looked down at my hand. My other eye popped open and my jaw dropped.

There was a brochure for Graceland in my palm.

"*Oh my God*, what does this mean?" I asked, hopeful, but unable to wrap my head around what I was holding in my hand.

"I talked with Dru and Tasha, they've got you covered. It'll be a couple months before school's out, but that gives us time to plan it all out, and then, we're going to Graceland, *Ba-by*!"

"*Oh my God*!" I squealed this time, jumping up and down three times before jumping into his arms and squeezing as hard as I could. "This is the best gift anyone has given me *in my life*."

Jackson laughed and said, "Good, that's what I was going for."

When I was back on my feet I looked at the brochure, hugged it to my chest, and told him, "You are getting so lucky tonight."

To which he replied, "I already am."

Gah, this guy . . .

Jackson

I was doing my best to wrangle two drunk, and one buzzed, sisters out of my truck and up the stairs to their apartments, without someone falling on their face. It wasn't as easy as one might think. These girls were wired and super affectionate. They kept stopping to hug each other, and me, then sat down on the steps when they deemed the climb too far.

"Come on, ladies, you'll feel better once we can get some aspirin and water in you, and you get in your comfy clothes," I cajoled, thinking the comfy clothes bit always worked on Kayla.

"Ohhhh, pajamas sound nice," Tasha cooed.

"Mmmhmmm, and these shoes *hurt*," Dru added, lifting her leg and kicking her foot until her shoe flew off, almost hitting me in the head.

Luckily, I caught it.

"Come on," Millie, the buzzed one, said, trying to help by pulling on her sister's arms. "Let's go get you changed."

"Hey," Dru said, pulling her arm out of Millie's grasp. "Not so rough, you'll leave a bruise." She turned toward me with a sloppy grin. "Maybe Jackson can carry me up; it is my birthday, after all."

"Oh brother," Tasha moaned with an exaggerated eye roll. "It's gotta be past midnight by now. This girl will milk her birthday until next year if you let her."

"No one is carrying anybody," Millie denied as she put Tasha's arm around her shoulder and they began taking it one step at a time. "Move your booty, Dru."

"She's so mean to me," Dru pouted, but she stood on wobbly legs and grasped the handrail.

I trailed behind them, ready to catch anyone who stumbled, until we reached the top.

We stopped in Tasha's apartment first, Millie taking her sister into the bedroom to get changed, while I looked for some type of aspirin and poured a glass of water. Mille came out, grabbed both from me, said, "Thanks," then disappeared back into the bedroom.

Once she came back out, we stepped out of the apartment, locked the door, and looked to the left to see Dru sitting on the floor in front of her door, her head tilted back against the wood and her eyes closed.

When she let out a soft snore, Millie giggled, then looked at me. "You hold her up, I'll open the door."

Millie entered the apartment, presumably to do exactly what we'd done at Tasha's as I strained to hold Dru's dead weight up and cross the threshold. Once we were inside, I heard a cough and a sniffle, then looked down to see Dru staring up at me.

"You okay?" I asked, hoping she wasn't about to puke on me.

"That guy who found your wife . . ."

"Mick," I supplied.

"Yeah, him . . . Do you think he could find our dad?" Dru asked, then her head fell forward and I had to brace myself before we both toppled.

Millie came out of the bedroom, some pajamas thrown over her arm, and said, "I've got her from here, why don't you head to my place and I'll meet you over there."

I accepted her keys with a nod, then left the sisters in peace, my mind running a mile a minute.

Millie had never mentioned her father. I was just now realizing none of them ever had. They'd spoken about their mom, what she was like, and how hard it was now that she was gone, but nothing about the man who was their father.

I was surprised that I'd never really thought about it, but now that Dru mentioned it, I was curious.

I was about to open Millie's door when I became aware of the discomfort I was feeling. Damn, these shorts were tight. And, I realized that I'd left my backpack with spare clothes in my truck. I jogged back down the steps as fast as the shorts would allow, grabbed what I needed, and headed back up to find Millie coming out of Dru's apartment.

"Is she all right?" I asked.

"Passed out," Millie replied with a smile. "But, I was able to get some Motrin and Gatorade in her first."

"That's good."

I used the key to open the door, then stepped aside to let her enter ahead of me.

When I would have headed straight to the bathroom to change, Millie turned and placed a hand on my chest.

"Uh-uh." She shook her head and guided me to stand in front of her couch, then went to the record player and messed with it until Elvis began crooning.

I watched as she took the headdress off and shook out her hair, then sat in front of me with a big smile.

"Entertain me, Elvis," Millie dared with a sexy smile, and my shorts got a whole lot tighter.

I flung my backpack onto the couch next to her, then began moving my hips as my fingers came up to first untuck my shirt at the waist, then unbutton it slowly. With my shirt hanging open, I did another pelvis thrust, which made Millie cat call and me turn red, then eased the shirt off my shoulders.

Millie's eyes widened, then narrowed and her face became flushed as she looked at my shorts. I looked down and saw that nothing was left to the imagination, as my dick strained against the thin fabric.

"C'mhere," she mumbled, her tongue darting out to wet her lips as she watched me step to her.

When I was close enough, Millie's hands reached out, grabbed me by the waistband, and tugged me closer, causing my blood to heat then boil when she started working on my zipper. And when she looked up at me from under her eyelashes, I was a goner.

Millie

I came awake slowly, my body thrumming as I was pulled from the darkness into the morning with a moan.

It took me a moment to register what was going on. First, I felt the yearning, then the pleasure, and finally, the sweet, wet heat of Jackson's tongue on me. I arched my back languidly with a moan as all of my senses awoke at once.

God, he's good at that, I thought briefly before I no longer had the ability *to* think.

As I came down, Jackson kissed one thigh, then the other, then dropped kisses on his way up my body. By the time he was fully on top of me, my arms were wrapped around him and I was smiling serenely up at him.

"Good morning," I whispered. And it was . . . what a great way to start the day.

"I wanted to do that last night, but we got a bit carried away," he began, causing me to moan at the memory of last night.

Me taking him in my mouth until he went wild, lost control, and bent me over the couch.

It had been amazing, frantic, and we'd been just buzzed enough to totally pass out afterward. Somehow, we'd at least made it to the bed before losing it, but we hadn't found the time to put on pajamas, so we were both still fantastically naked.

"Mmmm, I like the feel of you against me," I murmured, my hands roaming everywhere they could.

"And I love the feel of you beneath me," Jackson whispered before dropping his head to capture my lips with his.

I brought my knees up, then tilted my hips up.

"Are you sure?" he asked.

We'd already had the talk about being tested, birth control, and all of that. We were both clean and I was on the pill, so I answered, "Yes."

We both moaned as he slid inside of me, none of the urgency from last night present this morning. No, instead, it was like we were engaged in a sleek, sexy, Viennese Waltz, our bodies dancing in tune with each other.

"Nothing feels as good as this," Jackson said softly in my ear, before his lips moved down my neck, loving me there.

I shoved one hand in his hair and fisted it, matching his thrusts as I felt desire building within me again.

"You're the most amazing woman I've ever met," he panted, his breath becoming labored as he moved faster.

"So are you," I replied, not really knowing what I was saying as I felt the pressure begin to build.

Bracing my other hand on Jackson's shoulder, I held on and pushed up with my thighs so that my clit was in just the right spot as he moved over me. Then my whole body stilled as the orgasm crashed through me, and I was barely aware of Jackson shouting my name as he found his own release.

I grunted when he collapsed on top of me, so he apologized and rolled over to his side, taking me with him so that I was half splayed across his chest as we both struggled for breath.

After a few minutes, Jackson asked, "So, I'm the most amazing woman you've ever met?"

I was confused at first, then realized what I'd said in the heat of passion and started laughing so hard, I snorted.

"Sorry, I was a little preoccupied."

Jackson turned his head toward me, his dimples showing.

"I'll take that as a compliment."

"You should," I agreed, running my fingers across his ribs, causing him to flinch. "Sorry," I said, then tilted my head back and rested it against his bicep. "So, yesterday . . ."

Jackson closed his eyes briefly, then opened them and said, "I barely recognized her. Not just her personality, or the way she's been acting, but *physically*. She's lost a lot of weight, had work done . . . I guess when she said she needed to find herself, she actually meant to become a different person. I barely caught a glimpse of the Julie I knew."

"I'm sorry," I said, lamely, but what else *could* I say?

"Listening to her, seeing her, I got it . . . finally. A little. I mean, I don't understand it, and can't relate, but I finally understood what she meant."

"Wow, really?"

"Yeah, I mean, my heart was screaming that she's selfish, a horrible person, and a complete stranger." Jackson looked at me warily, as if worried I'd judge him for thinking bad things about his wife. When I nodded encouragingly, he continued, "But, in my head, I could see where she was coming from, and why she felt she needed to do what she did. That's not to say I condone it, or even forgive it, just that I get it."

"You're a good man," I assured him, thinking there was no way in hell I understood where she was coming from. Of course, I'd never even met her, let alone spoke with her, so how could I?

"You think?" he asked.

"Absolutely."

"Because even with all of that being said, I want to rip her heart out when I think about what she's doing to Kayla, what they're both missing out on." Jackson sighed and ran a hand over his face. "I have to talk to Kayla, tell her that I saw Julie."

"I'm so sorry, I can't imagine how hard that will be."

"It sucks. I've had to break her heart on Julie's behalf before, and I'm scared to see how she'll take it this time. But this is the last time I'm going to let her hurt our baby."

My heart hurt for both Jackson and Kayla as I thought about what it felt like to be abandoned by one of the people who was supposed to love you most. I knew what it was like, and I'd never been able to forget, or forgive. I could only hope that things would be different for Kayla.

Jackson

After a rocky afternoon yesterday, then an absolutely wonderful night, I picked up Kayla and decided to keep things light on the drive back.

I didn't want to have this discussion with her in the truck, but thought it would be best to be home, surrounded by our things, with easy access to her bed if she needed to lay down and cry it out.

Still, it was hard to be upbeat on the drive home, especially when the first thing Kayla asked when she got in the truck was, "Have fun with *Millie*?"

I decided to ignore her snide tone and answered, "Yes, I did."

Kayla'd crossed her arms and pouted the whole way home.

Once we got her things inside, unpacked, and put her dirty clothes in the laundry, I turned to my daughter and said, "We need to talk."

"I don't want to talk about Millie. You can't make me like her," she said snidely, and I had to remind myself that she was a nine-year-old girl who missed her mother and was about to be heartbroken once again.

It was hard, but I managed to keep that at the forefront of my mind and to put the issues with Millie on the backburner for now.

"It's not about Millie . . . for now," I warned, but kept my tone gentle, because I knew what was about to come. "Sit."

Kayla frowned and looked at me warily, but got up on her bed and sat against the pillows.

Once she was settled, I started, "I saw your mom yesterday."

When her face lit up, my heart shattered.

"Is she coming home?" Kayla asked hopefully.

"No, baby, she's not," I replied heavily.

Kayla's face dropped, then her eyes narrowed and she asked, "It's because you're seeing that Millie, isn't it? My mom would come home if you weren't going off on dates with someone else."

Shocked, I reared back, then gathered myself and stated, "No, Kayla, none of this has anything to do with Millie, so stop trying to blame her where there's no blame to be had. This has to do with your mother and me, and no one else."

Kayla crossed her arms and asked, obviously not believing me, "Then why isn't she coming home?"

On *home*, her tone wavered, and I knew she was trying not to cry.

I sighed, my heart heavy as I admitted, "Your mom is at a crossroads in her life. She's trying to find who she is and what she wants to be."

"But she's my mom, doesn't she know that?"

"Yeah, baby, she knows, but sometimes, maybe, not everyone is cut out to be a mom," I stated gently.

"But, she *is* a mom, she can't just quit."

Kayla's words echoed through my head, and oh, how I wished that were true, but the sad reality was that Julie had done exactly that. *Quit.*

"She'll always be your mom, but that doesn't mean she's going to be a part of our lives. She has a new life now, one that she likes, and doesn't want to come back to the one she left behind."

"What about me?" Kayla asked, unable to control the tears from spilling over any longer. "Doesn't she want me?"

"*Oh, baby*," I muttered, my own eyes filling at the utter sorrow in my daughter's voice. "She's a fucking idiot if she doesn't."

Kayla blinked, her mouth forming an O as she said, shocked, "Daddy, you said the F word. You never say the F word."

And I hadn't, at least not around Kayla . . . not ever. But if ever a time called for it, it was now.

"I'm sorry, K, but it's the truth. You're the most amazing, smart, funny, beautiful girl in the entire world, and if your mom can't see that, then she's a fucking idiot."

Kayla gasped and covered her mouth, then I heard the best sound ever, when she giggled.

"You just said it again."

I gave her a small smile, then held out my hands, closing them when she hurdled herself in and held her tight.

"I love you more than anything, Kayla."

"I know, Daddy, I love you, too."

We sat there, holding each other for I don't know how long, and although I was happy that she seemed to be doing okay, I knew it wasn't going to be that easy. Julie's leaving had gutted her the first time, and I had no way of knowing what the realization that she wasn't coming back, and didn't want to, was going to do to Kayla. All I could do was be there, and hope that would be enough.

"What do you say we order in pizza, then stuff our faces with ice cream while we watch the new superhero movie?"

"Okay," Kayla's said, her voice muffled by my shirt.

"Great, let's each get our pajamas on and I'll order the pizza while you get the movie ready."

Kayla nodded and let me go, but before I shut her door behind me, I turned and called, "K?"

"Yeah, Daddy?"

"We're going to be okay," I promised.

"I know," she said, giving me her bravest smile.

Millie

I'd heard the strain in Jackson's voice when he called after talking to Kayla, and as much as I wanted to rush over there and be a comfort to them both, I knew it would probably have the opposite effect, so instead, I stayed home with an aching heart.

Luckily, we'd all exchanged numbers with Ty, Rob, Rebecca, and Jan, so I'd been able to get a hold of Ty to find out when would be the best time, if any, to drop in and bring a surprise for Jackson.

I'd made a pineapple upside down cake, which Ty and Rob had agreed was Jackson's favorite, and was going to bring it by his classroom, along with a hug and maybe a quick kiss, to let him know I was thinking about him and was there if he needed anything.

Ty had assured me that there weren't any rules against visitors, and Jackson wouldn't get in trouble with the principal, or anyone else, if I stopped in.

I felt a little weird dropping in while he was at work, but our schedules were so busy, and I didn't feel right dropping by his house yet, so I figured this was my best bet. And, I promised myself I wouldn't get in the way or stay too long.

So, I told Ty, "Thanks," when he let me in and led me down to Jackson's class.

"No problem," Ty was saying. "I have a free period right now, and have some time before I have to set up for volleyball in the gym." We made a couple turns and I worried I wouldn't be able to find my way back out. "That was a dope party the other night."

"I'm glad you had fun," I said with a smile, hoping I didn't look too fussy in my blue floral dress with my hair pulled back in a tail. Dru had scoffed at me when I'd shown up to work wearing it, and had just rolled her eyes when I said I was dropping something off for Jackson really quick.

"Okay, so he's right in here. You can hold off until the bell rings if you want, or sneak in the back, totally up to you."

"Thanks, Ty."

"Anytime," he said with a grin, then jogged off down the hall.

I peered into the window of the door and saw Jackson standing at the front of the class. He looked adorable in his jeans and V-neck sweater, his glasses slightly askew and his hair messy like he'd been running his hands through it. He was currently lecturing and using his hands, a lot.

I let my eyes wander around the room, taking in the books lining shelves, the posters of movies that had been adapted from books and plays, and the way all of the kids' attention was rapt on their teacher.

These were teenaged kids. And, they weren't talking or texting, they were actually listening as he spoke.

I placed my hand on the knob and turned it gently, quietly, then pushed the door open just enough for me to hear what Jackson was saying.

"I know this is different than the books and plays we've read so far, but I assure you, it's not less romantic, angsty, or complicated than the others. *Little Women* is a classic for many reasons and people love it, and sometimes hate it, in profound and very personal ways. We're going to do this one a few Chapters at a time, then discuss. Well, sometimes discuss, other times, write . . ." This earned him a small groan, but the students were smiling when they did it. "We'll read through Chapter Five, which will introduce us to most of the major characters in the book, and discuss initial thoughts, feelings, and maybe even start a little bracket on how you all think things will go. At the end of the book, the winner will win some *Little Women* fandom items."

Some of the guys snorted at that, although, looking around the room, I realized the class was at least seventy-five percent girls. Which could be because of the subject matter, and not the handsome teacher at the head of the class.

I giggled at the thought, imagining how much I would have mooned over a teacher like Jackson Heeler as a young girl. Shoot, he made me swoon now, I couldn't even imagine what it would be like if I had raging hormones.

I looked back at Jackson, his dimples showing as his passion for his work shone through, and I knew that I'd officially fallen in the deep end.

Jackson was everything I'd ever wanted in a man, and *more*. He was the nuts on a sundae, the whipped cream on pecan pie, the salt on the salted caramel cupcake.

Jackson was the ingredient that turned a normal dish into something extraordinary, and *I am in love with him*.

The bell rang in the middle of my epiphany, startling me and causing my heart to jump.

I moved out of the way as kids starting barreling out of Jackson's classroom, and when the coast was clear, I slipped inside.

His back was to me as he organized something on his desk, so I cleared my throat and smiled as he turned.

Jackson's face lit with pleasure when he saw me.

"Hey, this is a nice surprise," he said as he met me in the middle of the room.

"Good," I said shyly, suddenly feeling just like one of those teenaged girls I'd just passed. "I wanted to check in on you and bring you this."

I lifted the bag containing his cake, then put my arms around him and added, "And, this."

"This is nice," Jackson murmured, hugging me back. He gave really good hugs, and I found I'd happily stand like this forever.

Of course, maybe that's my lovesick heart talking.

"What's in the bag?" Jackson asked when he reluctantly pulled back.

"Pineapple upside down cake. I have it on good authority that it's your favorite."

"It is," he said, his eyes lighting up. Then he looked at me mischievously and asked, "I don't have to share, do I?"

I laughed. "Not if you don't want to."

I swayed toward him and tilted my head back, and Jackson answered my request by giving me a soft, sweet kiss.

"I know you have class, and I have to get back to work, but I needed to check in on you," I admitted softly.

"I'm glad you did," Jackson assured me as he brushed a wayward hair off my cheek. "Seeing you always makes me happy."

"Good," I said with a grin, then started walking backwards toward the door. "I'll let you get back to it."

Jackson nodded, and I floated out the door and down the halls of the school.

Jackson

It had been a rough week.

Dealing with Julie's complete lack of desire to be a mom, and Kayla's reaction to it, along with a packed work schedule and the normal, everyday issues that never failed to pop up, I was exhausted.

Of course, being a single dad meant I couldn't give in to that exhaustion. Instead, it was Friday night and I was catching up on laundry, cleaning the floors, and putting away the dishes I'd been neglecting in the dishwasher.

To make matters worse, Kayla had gotten in trouble at school that day, and was currently sitting on her bed "thinking about what she did wrong."

My phone rang just as I opened the dishwasher, and I thanked whoever was calling for the distraction. Seeing it was my mother-in-law, I leaned against the counter and pressed answer, then greeted, "Hey, Ruth."

"Jackson, *she called*," Ruth said breathlessly, not even bothering to say hello.

I'd told her about finding Julie and what went down when I met with her, and although I could tell she was disappointed, I also knew that no matter what, Julie was her child, and she'd been anxious for any news about her, even if it wasn't what she'd hoped.

"That's great, Ruth, I'd hoped she would," I replied honestly.

"I'm going to see her next week, in Hampton."

"That's great, I'm happy for you. I know how much you've missed her." Everything I said was true, *still*, I couldn't help but feel bitter about the fact that Julie apparently had room for her parents in her new life, but not her daughter.

Refusing to dwell on it, I focused on what Ruth was saying.

"I tried to talk to her about Kayla, but she shut down, so I stopped. I'll try again when I see her," Ruth promised, and my heart ached for the older woman.

"Ruth, don't worry about it. I already spoke with Julie, and told her what needs to happen if she ever wants to be in Kayla's life. Just go and spend time with your daughter, without worrying about us."

"I don't know if I can do that, Jackson," she replied, and of course she couldn't. Ruth was a good woman. A great one, in fact.

"I know, I just mean, don't let it ruin your reunion. Get to know her again and maybe you can bring it up at a later date."

"All right, Jackson. And, thanks again for finding her, and for telling her to call us."

I heard Ruth begin to sob on the other end.

"No problem, Ruth."

"I love you, Jackson, and I'm so sorry for my daughter's actions."

"I love you too, Ruth, and like I've told you a million times, let Julie take ownership of her actions. You're an amazing grandmother. Have a good night."

"Good night," she responded softly, and I disconnected the phone.

I stared at my phone for a minute, before putting it down and opening the dishwasher, then closing it again and picking my phone back up.

How's your night? You done cooking for the baby shower?

Just texting Millie put a smile on my face and made me feel better. The woman really was good for me.

I put the phone back down and finally put off emptying the dishwasher. When I was done with the top rack, my phone dinged.

Yes, baby shower . . . check. Now I'm baking for tomorrow's Fiftieth Wedding Anniversary. You should see the pictures their kids sent me. #inspiring.

I grinned at her use of the hashtag.

You have time for a break at dinner?

I'd just put the last fork away and closed the dishwasher when she replied.

What are you bringing me?

My heart leapt at the thought of seeing her tonight, when I hadn't expected to.

Chinese or Sandwiches, your choice.

I wiped down the counters while I waited, snatching up my phone quickly when it chimed.

Chinese. Beef and Broccoli, please, with an egg roll.

You've got it, we'll be there soon.

Shoving my phone in my back pocket, I went to Kayla's room and knocked on her door once before opening it.

"Get your shoes and jacket, we're going to grab some dinner."

Kayla's face cleared, probably at the thought of being able to go out to eat, when she was supposed to be in trouble.

"Where are we going?" she asked, practically leaping off the bed.

"To pick up Chinese, then take it to Millie's work to have dinner with her."

Kayla landed with a thud and her face fell.

"Oh . . ."

"Yeah, oh, and you're going to be on your best behavior. None of this bratty, tantrum stuff you've been doing whenever Millie is around. You're a sweet, funny, *kind* girl, and I'd really appreciate it if you showed that side of you to my girlfriend."

The thundercloud on Kayla's face made me realize what I'd just said, and I groaned silently.

"*Girlfriend*?" she spat.

"That right there, that's exactly how I *don't* want you to act. Yes, she's my girlfriend," at least, I hoped she was . . . We hadn't ever really talked about it. "And I really like her. I think she likes me too, and I know she'd love you, if you'd just give her a chance."

When Kayla didn't respond, I lowered into a crouch and looked my daughter in the eyes.

"Can you please make an effort, K? For me?"

When she sighed and shrugged, I figured beggars couldn't be choosers, and took it.

Millie

He'd said *we'll be there soon*, and I doubted he meant Rob or Ty, or even Jericho, although I would have been less nervous with any of them . . . yes, even Jericho . . . than I was about his nine-year-old daughter who obviously hated me.

"It'll be fine, Millie," I assured myself out loud as I worked on the flowers for the various cakes that would be served at the anniversary party. Not fifty of them, thank goodness, although that would be cool, but each table would have their own cake centerpiece that would be a miniature version of the actual anniversary cake.

That meant I had a lot of flowers to make. Calla Lilies, which were the flowers she'd had in her wedding bouquet.

Still, when Jackson had offered to bring food, I'd jumped at the chance to see him.

"Talking to yourself again?" Dru asked as she walked in, her trusty clipboard in hand.

"Of course," I replied with a smile, then gave my sister a once-over and whistled. "Wow, you look great."

"I thought the baby blue would be a good fit for the baby

shower," Dru said, leaning up against the counter, her gaze on my hands as I worked on the flowers. "Plus, I wanted to show off the birthday shoes you and Tasha got me."

I glanced at her shoes briefly. "Sexy."

"I know, I love them," Dru gushed, then turned serious and asked, "Everything on track?"

I nodded and replied, "Claire and I loaded up, along with Enrique and Stacey, and the three of them took off to set up. Claire will come back after to see if I'm still working on the cakes, and the others will go home after breakdown."

"Perfect. I'm so excited about tomorrow. I heard that Mr. and Mrs. Stonopolis have written their own vows to renew and are going to be dressed to the nines. They are so sweet, and I can't wait to make their special day go off without a hitch. You should totally be on site for this one, Mills."

"I was thinking about it," I told her, a small smile playing on my lips. "You know I'm a sucker for a good love story."

"That's because you're in the middle of one," Dru joked, just as the bell chimed outside.

"You didn't lock up?" Dru asked with a frown, since the front was closed.

"Yeah. I just unlocked it for Jackson and Kayla; they're bringing me dinner."

Dru waggled her eyes at that, to which I had to reply, "*Shut up*," which was my sisterly duty.

"Hey," Jackson called.

"We're back here," I replied, taking a moment to flex my stiff hand.

"Hi, oh, hey, Dru," Jackson greeted as he walked in carrying a bag of food, his daughter trailing behind him wearing the sullen look I was beginning to think never faded.

"Hi, Jackson," Dru replied, setting down her clipboard and crossing to give him a side hug, then she looked down at Kayla and said, "And, you must be Kayla. I'm Dru, the cool twin."

Kayla looked momentarily surprised, heck, I think she almost even smiled, before saying, "I didn't know Millie had a twin. You guys look a lot alike."

"People have always said that, although we are fraternal, and I'm the pretty one . . ."

"Jerk," I said with a laugh.

Dru turned her head and winked at me.

"Actually, we have another sister, too. Tasha; she's the baby. We all work here together."

"Oh," Kayla responded, then closed her mouth swiftly and looked around the kitchen without saying another word.

"Are you hungry, Dru? We have plenty," Jackson offered, but Dru shook her head.

"Better not. I've got to head out, but you guys enjoy. Don't work too late, Mills," my sister ordered, then swept out of the room.

"I can take a break now," I said, rubbing my palm absently. "Want to eat at one of the tables out front?"

"Sure, come on, Kayla," Jackson replied, guiding Kayla back out the door they'd just entered, while I went to wash up and put a few things in the refrigerator.

When I was done, I found that he'd already set up the paper plates and had the cartons open and ready.

"I didn't know if you like anything else, so I got a few different items, but there's your Beef and Broccoli and the eggrolls. I also got some sauces and both forks and chopsticks." As he spoke, Jackson took the items out of the bag in his lap.

I grabbed the chopsticks and said, "Thanks, I really appreciate this. I hate to admit it, but I often get so caught up that I forget to eat."

"We're happy to feed you anytime, right, Kayla?" Jackson asked his daughter, trying to make her a part of the conversation, but all she did was shrug and keep her eyes on her plate.

Before I could think of something else to fill the silence, Jackson's phone rang. He looked down, frowned, then looked up at me and mouthed, "Lawyer," then stood up and walked back into the kitchen for some privacy.

"So, how was school this week?" I asked Kayla, painfully aware of how awkward things were with Jackson gone.

Shoot, they're awkward when he is in the room . . .

"Millie?"

I looked up to see Jackson standing in the doorway, motioning for me to come over.

I placed my chopsticks down and rose, then followed him out of the store.

"Is everything okay?" I asked when we were far enough that Kayla couldn't hear, assuming that if he wanted her to, he would have spoken to me at the table.

"That was my lawyer," he began, distracted as he fidgeted with his glasses. "He said that Julie is at his office right now and he wants me to come down."

"Why's she there?" I asked, my stomach dropping as a million different reasons crossed my mind.

"I don't know, he didn't want to go into it over the phone, just said I should get down there. He did say it's nothing major, so I'm assuming that means she's not contesting, still . . . I need to get down there and see what's up. I want to get this over and behind us so we can move forward."

"Of course, is there anything I can do?"

"Can K stay here with you?" he asked, and I was sure my worry shone through when he amended, "It'll only be for a little while, my lawyers' office is only like five minutes from here. I can't take her there and risk them bumping into each other, she can't handle that right now, and it would take too long to drive her to one of her grandparents. I won't be long, I promise."

"Yes, I'm happy to help," I said, but I couldn't help wondering how Kayla was going to react to this turn of events.

Jackson

I parked outside the lawyer's office and walked slowly in, giving myself time to try and calm down. To breath.

Mr. Hurley had said it wasn't bad, but the worry that had formed on my drive over was that Julie was going after Kayla. I remembered what she'd said just a few days ago, and I knew my lawyer would categorize such a thing in the *bad* category, but still, that's where my mind had wandered and stayed for the duration of my trip.

Now I was close to hyperventilating, I was so sure that Julie was about to try and take my baby away from me.

No way am I letting that happen, I promised myself as I opened the door and went into the waiting room. I turned my phone to silent, then crossed to the receptionist to let her know who I was and why I was there, then went to sit down. Before my butt could hit the chair though, my lawyer stepped out, and I knew he must have been waiting for me.

"Jackson," he called, giving me a welcoming smile, which eased my worry a tiny bit.

He wouldn't be smiling if my world was about to fall down around me, right?

We walked back into the hall, pausing outside the door to his conference room, and Mr. Hurley turned to me.

"Like I said on the phone, Julie showed up here asking to speak with me. She didn't have an appointment, so she waited about five hours until I could fit her in. My secretary didn't make the connection between you and Julie, since she has a different last name, and thought she was just a random walk-in, or I would have called you sooner."

I nodded that I understood, although I couldn't quite find my words yet. My throat was too dry, my heart beating too fast.

"Anyway, after speaking with Ms. Baker, I thought it would be best to call you in and try to handle this without paperwork, since yours is already being processed. No need to halt progress if it's not needed, right?"

I nodded again, tried for a smile, which felt more like a grimace, then followed him through the door when he opened it.

Julie was sitting at the end of the conference table, dressed somewhat demurely in a low-cut dress, at least, more demurely than last time I'd seen her. Her blonde hair was blown out and curled, and she wore light makeup. All in all, she looked quite pretty, although still completely opposite from the way she used to look.

It was almost hard for me to reconcile that she was the same woman.

I wanted to shout, to ask angrily, *what is going on?* Instead, I held my tongue, took the seat farthest from her, and waited with forced patience.

"First of all, I want to assure you that no changes to the divorce paperwork is necessary, rather this is just a meeting, in which I will mediate. It's a little out of norm, but as long as we get this done quickly and amicably, I have no problem with it. One of the nice things about owning your own law firm, is answering to no one but yourself; still, I wouldn't want this to become a habit," Mr. Hurley began, pausing so that each of us could process his words.

"Of course, thank you, I really appreciate your time," Julie said softly, because, apparently, I'd gone mute.

"Also, normally, Ms. Baker would have her own counsel. Since that is not the case today, I will reiterate that I am Mr. Heeler's lawyer, and am only here in the best interest of my client."

"Thank you," I managed to croak out, finally turning to Julie and asking, "What is this about?"

Julie twirled the ring on her middle finger nervously, then took a deep breath and brought her gaze to mine.

"I'd like my stuff," she said, and I blinked.

"What?" I asked.

That was the last thing in the world I'd been expecting her to say.

"My things . . . clothes, shoes, jewelry. The box of mementos from high school and when I was little. I'd like to set aside a time to box up and take my things, a time when you and Kayla aren't around."

My mouth was gaping like a fish as I stared at her.

"What?" she asked defensively. "It's *my* stuff, and I should be able to have it if I want."

"You came to my lawyer's office so that you could get your clothes?" I asked, my tone bordering on mean, but I couldn't help it, I was angry.

"Well, yeah. I didn't want to put my mom in the middle of it by asking her to ask you, and I didn't think showing up at the house unannounced was a good idea. This seemed like the safest way."

"*The safest way*?" I practically shouted. "Did you ever think of, I don't know, calling me?"

"I didn't think that was a good idea, and you did, *do*, seem pretty angry, so . . ."

"Oh, don't you pull that shit on me. *Angry*? You're damn right I'm angry, but you know I've never given you a reason to not feel safe around me, and although you're right, I'd rather you *not* call my phone, it makes more sense than having me called down to my lawyer's office for something that could have taken minutes to set up."

I took a deep breath and shook my head.

"I could give two shits about your *things*. What I'm so angry about, is that you're more worried about some fucking shoes and mementos, than your own daughter . . ."

"Jackson," Mr. Hurley warned, and I took another deep breath before muttering, "Sorry."

"Yes, we can set up a time for you to come pack up and take your things, and no, Kayla certainly won't be there. But I will be. There's no way you're going into *my* home without me being present."

"Okay," Julie said softly.

I rose quickly and added, "Now, if that's all, I need to get back to my daughter. Text me to set up a time to get your things." Then I turned my attention to Mr. Hurley and said, "I'm sorry for wasting your time. Thanks for your patience."

Then I got the hell out of there.

Millie

We'd finished eating in silence after Jackson left, my Beef and Broccoli tasteless, so I barely ate at all.

After we cleaned up, I took Kayla into the back. I gave her a brief tour, making sure she knew where the bathroom was, showing her our office, the kitchen, and the different walk-ins. I thought briefly about taking her up into my apartment, so she could hang out and watch TV or something, then figured it was too far and maybe for my first time watching her, I should keep her close.

So, we were in the kitchen and I was explaining the flowers I was making, the type of cake it would go on, and telling Kayla about the party the next day. If there was ever a person who looked or acted more bored, I'd never met them. Still, I kept trying.

"You can make flowers with frosting, fondant, gum paste . . ."

"He's never going to fall in love with you, or marry you, you know," Kayla broke in, her tone full of anger.

I looked up from what I was doing, put my tools down, and started as gently as I could, "*Kayla . . .*"

"No, this is stupid. My dad loved my mom, and she left us, she's never coming back. So now, he has me, and we're doing just fine. We were happy and everything until you showed up. Now you think you can take him away, but you can't. He told me, I'll always be his number one girl . . . *not you.*"

My stomach clenched painfully as the anger on Kayla's face turned to worry and sadness.

"Oh, honey, I'm not trying to take your place, or your mother's. I really like your father, and we're having a great time getting to know each other, that's all it is right now. No one has said anything about marriage or anything, so you don't need to get worked up about that. Not now, let's just get to know each other, okay? I think that would really make your dad happy."

For some reason, my words brought the anger back. In fact, Kayla looked so angry, with her red face and clenched fists, that it made me worried for her.

"You don't know what makes him happy," she spat.

I lifted up my hands and spoke softly, hoping to calm her down.

"You're right, let's just take a break, maybe go in the back and have some water."

"I don't want to go anywhere with you. I don't want you coming to my house for tacos, I don't want to come here to your stupid kitchen to watch you make stupid food. I want you to leave us alone!" she shouted, and before I knew her intentions, she rushed to my counter, lifted her arm, and swept all of my flowers onto the floor. *"I hate you."*

My heart was pounding and my hands were sweating, and I felt utter despair as I looked at all of my hard work in a crumbled heap on the ground.

"Go back to my office and wait for me there. I'll come back when we've both calmed down," I managed to say through my teeth.

When it looked like Kayla might argue, I said more sternly, "Now!"

Kayla huffed in response, but followed my directions and stomped off toward my office. After a few moments, I heard the door slam, then braced myself against the counter with my hands.

I tried breathing in through my nose and out through my mouth, but it didn't work. My eyes filled with tears anyway as I thought about the confrontation we just had, then about how long it was going to take to redo all of the work I'd already completed.

It's going to be a long night.

I used my sleeve to wipe the tears from my cheeks, then went to the refrigerator and pulled out two waters.

You can do this . . . you know what she's going through and can put yourself in her place. She's hurting and took it out on you, but you're a grown woman, you can take it.

Once I was done with my mental pep talk, I squared my shoulders and went to the office. Opening the door, I held the waters in front of me, like a peace offering, then faltered when I saw that Kayla wasn't there.

I set the waters down on Dru's desk and did a quick search of the room, looking under all the desks and in the closet.

Nothing.

I started calling out, "Kayla," as I left the office and searched all of the walk-ins, the bathroom, the kitchen, and the storefront.

When I didn't see her and she didn't answer, I ran up the stairs to the apartment level and tried all of our doors. They were all locked, so I knew she couldn't have gotten in. Panic started setting in as I whirled in the hallway and ran back down the stairs.

I did another lap around the downstairs, hoping like hell Kayla was hiding from me, but when she didn't come out and didn't call out, I grabbed my phone and dialed Jackson.

"You have reached the voicemail of Jackson Heeler," the automation said after a few rings, his voice supplying his name.

I waited for the beep and said, "Call me as soon as you get this."

I pressed end, cursing under my breath as I retraced her steps from the mess in the kitchen, down the back hall, and to our office. That's when my eyes caught on the door at the end of the hallway.

The back exit.

I rushed to the door, pushing it open so hard it slammed against the wall as I looked out over the back parking lot, only to find it empty.

She's gone.

Jackson

There was a war of motions happening within me. A fight between annoyance and relief.

It was annoying that Julie had reentered my life only to gather her *things*, but a total relief that she wasn't contesting the divorce and it was still going through on schedule. I needed that part of my life to be in the past, needed to move forward, needed to be able to focus on the fall with Millie.

So, I was cruising down Main Street, feeling pretty good, even if I did have another meeting with Julie looming.

I pulled up to the curb in front of Three Sisters and was hopping out of the truck, eager to get back inside and see my girls, when Millie came rushing around from the back of the building, crying and visibly shaking as she called out for Kayla.

My heart leapt out of my chest as fear coursed through me.

"Millie!" I shouted, jogging over to her on the sidewalk.

Her head was turning quickly from side to side as she searched the street, and she was so caught up in her panic that my return didn't immediately register.

When I was almost to her, I called her name again, then reached out and touched her shoulder. "What's going on?" I asked. "Where's Kayla?"

"I don't know . . ." Millie cried, her head still swinging back and forth, obviously out of her mind with worry, which was really freaking me out. "She got mad, threw my flowers, and we fought . . . *I don't know what makes you happy, I can't take her place* . . . I told her to go cool down, but she left." I understood the gist of what she was saying, but not all of it. "I went to take her a water and she was gone . . . just *gone*."

"She couldn't have gone far," I began, adrenaline rushing through me as I thought of all the possible terrors my daughter could be facing. "You checked the whole place, upstairs and down?" Millie nodded as she still frantically searched the streets. "What about businesses, have you asked any of them?"

"Not yet, I just came outside when I realized that she left. Then, you were here."

"Okay," I said, thinking at least Kayla hadn't been gone long. "Let's split up and check the stores. You go down this way and I'll cross the street."

Millie took off before I'd even finished my sentence, so I started to run across the street, when I heard someone shout my name.

"Jackson."

My head whipped in the direction of the sound, and I saw Jericho standing outside Prime Beef, waving me over.

"Kayla's here!" he shouted, and I practically tripped over my feet with relief.

I turned to call out to Millie, but saw her standing still on the sidewalk, tears streaming down her face as she watched us.

"I tried to call you, but your phone kept going straight to

voicemail," Jericho was saying as I got closer. "It just hit me that she was probably coming from your girl's place, so I was coming over to see if you were there. She's fine, I got her settled in before coming out to find you. I hope you weren't too worried."

"Thanks, man, I turned my phone to silent when I was with my lawyer, and forgot to turn it back."

I turned back to see if Millie was joining us, but found the street empty. I hoped she was okay, but seeing how distraught she'd been, I figured she needed a minute.

"Can you take me to her?" I asked, thinking I'd grab her then we'd go back to check on Millie, and Kayla would have a lot of apologizing to do.

"Yeah," Jericho said, clapping me on the back before leading me into his restaurant, through the dining room and into the kitchen.

My gaze took in the chaos, before landing on my daughter set up in the back.

They'd pulled up a barstool, given her a piece of cake and glass of milk. Her head was down as she drew on the paper Jericho had given her, so she didn't see me approach. I felt a quick rush of relief that she was safe and sound, followed by a flash of anger as I remembered that panic on Millie's face.

She'd thought my daughter was in danger, and the reality that Kayla was sitting here like she was having the time of her life made me angrier with her than I'd ever been.

"Kayla."

My tone had Kayla jumping in her seat, and she turned to me with a smile and a, "Hi, Daddy," before she registered the look on my face and the smile fell.

"Get up," I ordered, and I saw her gaze swing to Jericho before she slid off the stool and walked slowly toward me. I turned to

Jericho and said, "Thanks for looking out for her. I'm sorry if she was in the way."

"Not at all," my buddy replied. "I'm here for you."

I nodded, then pointed toward the door and told Kayla, "Go."

I walked behind her, trying to calm down before I said something that I'd regret, but I was so angry and disappointed in her, and those were emotions I'd never felt for my daughter before. Not on that level.

Once we got outside and I looked around to make sure we didn't have an audience, I turned to Kayla with a frown.

"I am beyond disappointed in you, young lady. You know better than to run off like that, you're nine years old, not four." I watched Kayla's shoulders sag and fought the guilt at making her feel bad. "Millie was out of her mind with worry. She didn't know if you were hurt, taken, or worse . . . You need to go over there right now and apologize. For everything. Whatever you did to her flowers, for arguing with her, saying mean things, and disappearing. You probably need to make it up to her somehow . . . I don't know, I'll talk to her. Maybe you can clean up the kitchen or something."

Kayla's chin began to quiver as her eyes filled.

"I'm sorry, Daddy . . ."

"Save it for Millie," I said, then put my hand on her shoulder and guided her across the street.

When we went into the front area, then the kitchen, where I saw the beautiful flowers Millie had been working on broken in a heap on the floor, I looked at Kayla and saw her wince. When we didn't see Millie, we went upstairs and knocked on her door.

After a few moments, I heard movement behind the door. When the door didn't open, I knocked again, and waited.

Finally, the door opened slowly and Millie peered out, her face swollen and puffy from crying, but before I could apologize, she looked from Kayla, then to me and stated, "I'm sorry, I can't do this . . ."

Millie

"What do you mean?" Jackson asked, his face conveying his confusion.

I looked pointedly from him to Kayla and whispered, "Now's not the time . . ."

Jackson looked down at his daughter, who was watching me with a shocked expression, then brought his gaze back to mine and stated, "I'll be back."

I watched numbly as he grasped Kayla and started walking her away from my door and down the hall. I noticed Kayla still watching me as I quietly shut the door, crossed to my chaise, and resumed the position I'd been in.

Fetal.

Sobs erupted again as decades-old sorrow filled me, compounded by the fresh pain I was feeling now.

It felt like only moments before rapid knocking sounded at the door, like gunfire to my heart, and I rose, my stomach sinking at the thought of what I was about to do.

What I had to do . . .

I opened the door without looking, without waiting to acknowledge who was there, and spun on my heel to go back to my couch, my safe haven. I crawled back on my chaise, pulled a throw pillow on my lap, and hugged it, along with my knees, to my chest, as a sort of armor. Only then did I force my eyes to see Jackson, who'd grabbed the tissues off my table and was holding them out to me.

His kindness only made me cry harder.

"Jesus, Millie," Jackson bit out, his hand going through his hair so hard he was practically pulling it. "What is going on?"

I did my best to pull myself together, realizing that the faster I got this over with, the faster he would be gone, and I would no longer have to face his perfection in person, I would only be left with the reminder.

Once I felt capable of forming sentences, I used one tissue to mop up my face, then another to blow my nose, before taking a deep breath and starting straight ahead as I spoke.

"Kayla isn't ready for this," I began, my voice hoarse. "I should have known when we started. I guess I did know, at least I'd had reservations about you still being married . . . but I should have known that Kayla wasn't ready for you to seriously date anyone else."

"*Millie,*" Jackson began, obviously upset and wanting to contradict what I was saying, but I kept talking.

"Please, let me get this out."

When he was silent, I continued, "She hates me. I mean, not *me*, because she doesn't know me, but she hates the thought of me. Of what I represent. First her mom left, now it's just been confirmed that she doesn't have any plans to come back, so, of course, Kayla is going to latch even harder on to you, and view anyone who could compete with her for your attention as a threat. She needs time . . ."

I could tell Jackson was biting his tongue. He wanted to speak so badly that he was squirming in his seat next to me, but being the wonderful man that he is, he respected my wishes.

Shit.

I took another deep breath.

"When we were little, our dad cheated on our mom, then left us to be with the other woman and never came back. He didn't say goodbye, or tell the three of us anything, and we've never heard from him again. Tasha was angry, kind of like Kayla is now, while Dru pretended nothing happened. *I*, was devastated. I was Daddy's little girl, one hundred percent." I was barely whispering now, caught back up in the memories. The pain. "He used to take me everywhere with him. To work, fishing, poker night, to all his favorite restaurants. He's the one who introduced my love of food. When my mom told us that he'd left, I didn't believe her at first. My daddy wouldn't do that, so I waited. I waited, and waited, and waited, and he didn't come back. That first day I slept on the front porch, my mom crying with me as she held me in her arms."

Jackson scooted a little closer, then stopped, and I knew he was having a hard time keeping his distance.

I turned my face toward him and finally looked in his eyes. He was hurting for me. With me.

"Then I blamed my mother. I was awful to her, just horrible, and she took it. She kept being there for me, holding me while I screamed and cried. Eventually, I became numb. I stopped waiting, stopped looking for him everywhere, and told everyone at school that he'd died. I guess in a way, to me, he *was* dead."

After a few moments of silence, Jackson finally spoke up and said, "I'm so sorry, Millie. How old were you?"

I held his gaze as I replied, "Eight."

Jackson nodded, understanding my point.

"I'm sorry that you went through that, and you were in so much pain, but did it have any bearing on what you felt for your mom when she started dating again?" he asked.

I smiled sadly and shook my head.

"She never did. My mom never went on a date, never brought a man over to meet us, heck, she never even kissed anyone else. He broke her completely. She gave us ninety nine percent of herself for the rest of her days on this earth, but that one percent was always reserved for *him*."

"Again, I'm sorry, and I understand your pain, your reservations, but *this* isn't *that*," Jackson argued as he moved just a little closer.

"Yes, you've been separated for a year, but you kept your ring on and your home exactly the same as it had been when your wife was there. I bet all of her things still hang in the closet." I paused, and when he didn't protest, I knew I was right. "The divorce isn't even completed yet, and you and I are hurtling pretty quickly toward a serious relationship. You may be ready for that, but Kayla isn't. She was still hoping that her mom was going to come home, and she needs more time to come to terms with the fact that Julie isn't, before she can open herself up to a new woman in your lives."

"Millie, look, everything your saying has merit," Jackson said as he stood and began pacing, his tone frantic. "But Kayla will be okay. I'll talk to her, and we can ease her into it slowly . . ."

"There's nothing you can say right now that will change my mind," I said sadly, my eyes filling once again.

Jackson stopped and crouched in front of me, his hands covering mine gently.

"Not even that I'm in love with you?" he asked, causing my heart to shatter.

I swallowed the lump in my throat and shook my head.

"Not even that," I managed, then turned my head and shut my eyes, not opening them again until I heard my door softly shut behind him.

Jackson

Zombie.

That was my new persona . . . A dead man walking.

I had never, not when I was a teenager, not when my wife said she was leaving, felt the way I did when Millie said my love wasn't enough.

Suddenly the literature I taught, the poems I'd read, the songs I heard on the radio, all took on new meaning. Hurtful, heartbreaking, painful meaning.

I'm not sure how I drove home, made it through the night, and then the rest of the week. I know I'd gone to work, because I had papers to grade, and I knew I'd taken care of Kayla. Helped her with her homework, made her meals . . . although I couldn't eat. I didn't have the appetite for it. And I knew I hadn't slept.

No, I'd spent the last four nights staring at my ceiling, fighting the urge to call her and beg her to change her mind, my time with Millie playing on a loop like some awful romantic comedy.

The first time I saw her walk out of the kitchen, the day I went there to beg for a tea party.

The way she'd transformed my dining room into a nine-year-old's dream.

Millie laughing at Rob and Ty in the teacher's lounge.

The way she'd looked after our first kiss, while laughing, when I moved inside of her.

She was everywhere . . . In my house, in my truck, at my school. There was no escaping the curve of her lips, the soft length of her neck, the way she'd looked in that flapper dress.

I was obsessed. *Possessed*. Unable to be present in any situation.

"Daddy," I heard Kayla call, and struggled to come back to the surface and see what she needed.

I blinked, and looked down at my daughter. I noted that she'd eaten her breakfast, *okay, so it's morning*, and that she had on her backpack, *which means it's a school day and I need to go to work*.

"Yes, baby?" I asked, pushing back from the counter I'd been leaning against and putting down the cup of coffee I'd held in my hand, but was still full.

"Are you almost ready to go?" Kayla asked softly, her worry for me apparent.

I tried for a smile, which was probably more of a grimace, and said, "Yeah, just give me a minute."

"Okay, Daddy."

Kayla had been on her best behavior over the last few days. At first, when I'd come home from Millie's, she'd been worried about how much trouble she was going to be in, but even though I'd tried to put on a brave face, she'd seen I was upset for a different reason.

Since then, she'd been attentive, helpful, and sweet.

I knew I needed to get over this funk soon, and stop allowing my daughter to comfort me, but I wasn't there yet. Although, I promised myself as I threw on some jeans and a T-shirt that I would be soon.

"All ready," I said, hoping I sounded chipper as I walked out of my room.

"Can I go to Grandma's tomorrow?" Kayla asked once we were in my truck.

I glanced at my daughter and asked, "You want to?"

"Yes, please," she said softly, her head turned toward the window.

"Of course you can," I assured her, guilt hitting me.

Shit, I'm being such a drama queen, my own daughter doesn't want to be around me.

I dropped her off, making a point to give her a hug, *so she knows I love her*, but not a kiss, *so I don't embarrass her*, then watched her rush over to her friends and start talking happily, and smiled my first real smile in days.

See, I'm going to be okay.

Of course, then I got to the high school, which is like a real-live love fest. Kids kissing in the hall, against their lockers, out in the parking lot. And during lunch, not only did I imagine Millie dropping in with cake, but I had to see Rebecca and Ty making goo goo eyes at each other.

Sure, I was happy for them, but right now it was more of a happy with finger quotes, than true happiness.

Mostly I was just envious.

Rob watched me nervously as he ate his turkey sandwich on wheat, as if worried I'd burst out crying at any moment.

For the record, I hadn't cried once, I'd just had something in my eye at one point.

I trudged down the hall, ready for the day to be over, and tried not to glare at the lovesick teens as I passed. When I entered my room, I was surprised to see my desk covered with a myriad of Little Debbie's snack cakes.

I'm talking Cosmic Cupcakes, Banana Twins, Honey Buns, Strawberry Shortcake Rolls, and my favorite, Star Crunch.

Once everyone was seated and class was about to begin, I turned to my students and asked, "What's all this?"

At first no one said anything, then one of the girls, Jeannie, spoke up.

"We noticed you were upset and heard about you and your girlfriend, so we thought you needed a little food therapy. It worked when I broke up with Sergio last month, and with Vic and Tamara."

I was touched, even as embarrassment flooded me over being so transparent. I really had been sucking at life over the last few days.

"What do you say we change things up today? Read from a different sort of classic," I asked, picking up my tablet as I leaned back against my desk and tore open a Star Crunch with my teeth. "A little story called, *The Shining*."

Millie

I was going through the motions.

I'd been working on autopilot since Jackson walked out of my apartment. Wake up, shower, shuffle downstairs, cook, bake, clean, sleep, repeat. Luckily, we were fully staffed and Claire had become my right hand, so we hadn't missed any deadlines, and when I'd made chicken and dumplings instead of chicken pot pie, Claire had fixed things in time for the event.

Dru had come to me only seconds after Jackson left, saying her twin vibes had been tingling and she'd known that I needed her. Soon after, Tasha'd shown up, and the two of them had been my shadows ever since. Even going so far as to sleep in my apartment each night.

I'd felt heartbreak when my dad left, but nothing like what I was feeling with the absence of Jackson in my life. Never pain so acute. And the worse part was that I knew I'd caused Jackson the same amount of pain. Even if I felt like I was doing it for the right reasons, I still hated the thought of him hurting.

I'd never been so emotionally invested in someone other than my family, but Dru kept assuring me that things would get better, although the look on Tasha's face when Dru said that had me thinking that Tasha still felt the pain of losing Jericho . . . and that had been years ago.

I'm screwed. Left to stew in the misery of my own making.

"I'm running to meet with a new prospective client," Tasha said as she came up behind me and hugged my back.

I kept whipping my meringue, but acknowledged her with a nod.

"And I have that interview with the radio station in an hour, so I'm going to go get ready," Dru added, before kissing my cheek.

"Go, keep expanding our business," I ordered, starting to feel suffocated by their hovering. "I'll be fine here. I've got plenty to keep my busy all day, and well into the night."

"Okay, but call us if you need anything," Tasha said.

I rolled my eyes and bit back the, *yes, mother*, that was threatening to come out. Instead, I just nodded again, then held my breath until they left.

Once they were gone, I could breathe again and proceeded to lose myself in my work, thankful for the menial task of whipping meringue. It didn't take a genius to make the delicious topping that would adorn my lemon meringue pie, just a few simple ingredients, some patience, and a strong wrist.

I opted to make the meringue by hand instead of with a mixer, for this very reason. So I could lose myself in the creation.

"Hey, Millie."

It took me a moment to register my name being called and pull myself out of the numbness. After a few seconds, I turned my head toward the sound and blinked at Claire.

"Yes?"

"You have a woman out here asking for you."

Claire was manning the storefront this morning, as she had for the last five mornings, allowing me to hide in the back.

I blinked again, then looked down at my meringue, still whisking, and said, "About two more minutes."

"I'll let her know," Claire replied, and I focused back on the task at hand.

Once the meringue was finished, I put it aside with the intention of finishing the pie once I was done talking to whomever was waiting out front, washed my whisk, then finally my hands, before checking my apron for stains and heading out of the kitchen.

I glanced at Claire, who tilted her head to her right. I started toward the older woman who was standing by the display case. She was well-dressed, with her hair and makeup done. She had a kind, open face, but I'd never seen her before.

Thinking she was here to put in an order or see about booking a party, I tried my best to put my professional face on as I approached.

"Yes, ma'am, how can I help you today?"

Her gaze swung away from the pastries before her and locked on my face, assessing, before her lips parted and she said, "Hello, Millie, right?"

"Yes, I'm Millie," I stated, holding my hand out.

She placed her well-manicured hand in mine and said, "Nice to meet you, I'm Rhonda Heeler."

Her last name slapped me in the face so hard that I flinched and started to pull my hand from her grasp, but for a small woman, she was strong, and tightened her grip.

"My granddaughter asked me to bring her here today." At the mention of Kayla, I started to survey the dining area, then noticed movement behind Mrs. Heeler and watched as Kayla stepped out from behind her. "Is there somewhere we could talk?"

"Ah, yes, of course, please, follow me," I managed, finally getting my hand back and turning to lead them through the kitchen and to the stairs up to my apartment. I didn't look back to make sure they followed, *rude of me, I know*, but I needed the time to compose myself.

To say I was shocked would be an understatement. Not only that Kayla had sought me out, but this was not the way I saw my first meeting with Jackson's mother going. Being here with Kayla, she had to know what had happened between Jackson and me, at least the gist of it. What must she think of me?

I motioned to my kitchen table. It was small, but probably the best setting for whatever this was.

"Can I get you anything?" I asked automatically, my mother's insistence on hospitality shining through. "Water, coffee, some cookies?"

"No thank you," Mrs. Heeler said, at the same time Kayla requested, "Cookies."

I couldn't stop my small smile at Kayla. Even thought our last encounter had been disastrous, I really did empathize with her.

I put the chocolate macadamia nut cookies on a small serving plate and placed it in the center of the round table, then with nothing left to do, I sat. My chair made a loud scraping sound as I tried to get comfortable, then I breathed a cleansing breath in through my nose, folded my hands on the table in front of me, and tried to look poised.

From the smile on Mrs. Heeler's face, she could see right through me, but was too polite to comment on it.

I was looking to Mrs. Heeler to start the conversation, but it was Kayla who said, "I'm sorry, Millie."

I blinked back a rush of tears as my throat burned at the sadness in her voice.

Turning my attention to Jackson's daughter, I could see she had a lot weighing on her young mind, so I bit my tongue and waited for her to finish what she wanted to say.

Kayla took a deep, exaggerated breath, and blew it out. She picked up a cookie and broke a piece off, but didn't put it in her mouth. Finally, she tore her eyes from the table and looked at me.

When she didn't speak right away, Mrs. Heeler put her hand on her granddaughter's shoulder, then looked at me and explained, "Kayla and I had a long talk about her feelings and the way she's been behaving. It was her idea to come here to talk to you, so she could apologize."

With that said, she gave Kayla a nod of encouragement.

"I was awful to you," Kayla began, her eyes holding mine bravely. "Rude and mean, and running away that day was *in-un-ah . . .*" She looked to her grandmother for guidance.

"Unforgivable," Mrs. Heeler coached, her tone firm, but her eyes gentle.

"Yeah, unforgivable. I never should have broken your flowers or yelled at you. It wasn't really even you I was mad at." Kayla looked to her grandmother once more, and when she nodded, finished with, "It was my mother. It *is* my mother . . . that I'm mad at, not you."

Needing to ease her burden, I reached my hand out and placed it on her forearm.

"I understand, and I promise, I'm not mad at you, Kayla. I was really worried when I couldn't find you," I amended. "But, I'm not angry with you, and I do understand how you're feeling. When I was little, my dad left us, and although it's not exactly the same as what you're going through, I do understand why you were upset."

"You're not mad at me?" she asked softly, her eyes on my hand on her arm.

"No."

"And, your dad left?"

"Yes."

"But, you're mad at my dad?"

Her question made my heart skip a beat.

"No, honey, I'm not mad at him."

Kayla lifted her head, bringing those eyes that were so much like Jackson's to mine and holding.

"Then why aren't you talking to him? If you're not mad at me, and you're not mad at him, what's going on? He's very sad, and he misses you. You should call him."

Unsure of how to react, and having the distinct feeling that I was being played, I looked to Jackson's mother like she could be my lifeline. She wasn't.

"I've never seen him so upset," Mrs. Heeler said pointedly, and I knew she was referring to Julie, but didn't want to bring up the other woman in front of Kayla.

I looked from grandmother to granddaughter, then back again, unsure of how to proceed. What to do. How to feel.

"I don't know if the timing is right . . ." I began, but Mrs. Heeler held and got right to the point.

"Do you love him?"

I gulped, unsure of how truthful I should be.

"My daddy says, either you love someone or you don't. I heard him in class one time, and he said the characters in his books spend so much time being *ob-ob* . . . What's the word for dumb?" she asked.

Mrs. Heeler and I both said, "*Obtuse*."

"Yeah, *obtuse*. The characters spend so much time being obtuse, that they miss out on all kinds of good times with the person they love. That if you're in love, you should tell the person, and you'll both be happier."

"*Ah* . . ." I croaked, unable to get words to come out of my mouth.

"It's okay," Mrs. Heeler said as she rose, pausing to pat my hand gently. "We came here to say what we needed to say, what you do with it, is up to you."

They crossed the room to my front door, leaving me sitting at my table, gaping. Then, with one hand on the door handle, Mrs. Heeler looked over her shoulder at me and added, "You look like a smart woman, Millie. I hope my instincts about you are correct."

And with that, they swept out of my apartment, leaving me staring after them, wondering what the heck just happened, and *what I'm going to do about it*?

Jackson

Another Monday, another workday, another day where I was just passing through life. Not really living it, instead floating from minute to minute, waiting for the day to end.

I'd been in such a funk that I was starting to get on my own nerves, and as I walked through my classroom, making sure my students were focused on their own quizzes and not peeking at anyone else's, I vowed to sort my shit out that evening.

Maybe I'll ask the guys to go out for a drink.

As if I'd conjured him, I saw Ty's face pop up in the window to my door. I held up a finger to indicate I couldn't talk now, but would get back to him later. Rather than nod in response as usual, he got this big goofy grin, gave me two thumbs up, and pushed my door open.

What the . . . ?

I stopped in the middle of my room when Millie stepped through the door he'd just opened, a piece of loose-leaf paper clutched in her hands.

I drank in the site of her like a man drowning. The soft billowy curls of her chestnut hair, the way the pretty floral dress accented her delicate curves and flowed down to her sandaled feet. She looked gorgeous, but the way I'd been missing her, she could have walked in wearing a burlap sack and she would have been the best thing I'd ever seen in my life.

Even as my heart roared back to life, I stopped myself from rushing forward and taking her in my arms.

I need to be smart, and guard myself. After all, I couldn't be certain of why she was here.

"Millie, uh, hi, what are you doing here?" I asked, trying to come off as unconcerned, but ruining it when my voice cracked.

"I needed to see you," she began softly.

"I'm in the middle of class, maybe we can get together after school," I suggested, even though the last thing I wanted was for her to leave. Still, I couldn't come off as totally eager. I didn't want her to think I'd been pining like some lovesick teen, even though that was an accurate description.

I need to be a man.

"I'll only take a moment," Millie argued, her tone wavering.

I watched her take a deep breath and noticed the paper shaking slightly in her grasp, and was about to say *fuck manhood* and go to her when she stopped me in my tracks.

"What greater punishment is there in life when you've lost everything that made it worth living?"

Her voice was strong as she read off the page, and I heard my class begin to murmur.

"Shakespeare," one of my kids whispered to the class, and I was proud that they remembered.

"I'm so sorry," Millie was saying, her eyes back on me. "I was scared. Terrified actually. And losing Kayla that way, seeing how she was dealing with everything that's going on in her life right now, brought back all of these feelings that I hadn't had in years, and I freaked out."

I waited, needing to hear more.

She looked back down.

"It is better to lose your pride to the one you love, than to lose the one you love, for your pride."

At the word *love*, my world stopped and through the buzzing in my ears, I heard another student say, a little louder this time, *"Pride and Prejudice."*

I looked around the room and saw we had my students' undivided attention. There were smiles and faces resting on palms, one kid was even taking notes. If someone pulled out a bowl of popcorn, I wouldn't have been surprised.

"I was afraid, a total chicken, and I know that's not what you *or* Kayla need in your lives, but I promise it won't happen again. I realize that I can help Kayla get through this, not only because I've been through it, but because I care about her. About her happiness. And, when she and your mom came to see me, I knew that we'd be able to get through this time together."

"My mom and Kayla came to see you?" I asked, remembering Kayla's insistence on going to my parents.

Sneaky girl.

Millie cleared her throat nervously, bringing my attention back to her.

"When I look into your eyes I don't see just you. I see my today, my tomorrow and my future. For the rest of my life."

"I don't think I know that one," one of the guys said.

After a few seconds, someone, I think Jeannie said, "Oh, *oh*, I think it's *Outlander*."

I saw Millie smile a little and decided that Jeannie deserved an A for reading more than the required reading for class.

"I've never felt the things I feel for you, for anyone else, and I never will. I know I got scared and messed up, and I'm sorry for the pain I put you through, but I hope you can forgive me. Give me another chance."

I didn't move, not to nod or give her any sort of affirmation. It wasn't just that I was stunned, although I was, and it wasn't that I was wary, although I was that, too. It was that I was positively swooning.

Swept off my feet.

Knocked to my knees by this woman who was turning my life into one of the very books she was quoting, the books that were my passion, my work . . .

"My heart is, and always will be, yours."

Her hands dropped to her sides, the paper hanging from her fingers. The paper that I would take from her and frame, to show all of our children, grandchildren, and their children after.

"*Sense and Sensibility*!" Jonathon shouted out, obviously pleased to have figured one out first.

I tuned him out and finally crossed to her.

Millie's head tilted back as she looked at me with hopeful eyes. "I'm gonna need that paper," I said, before sealing our fate with a kiss.

I tried to ignore the cheering and catcalls of my students, but when I broke the kiss and pulled back, we were both grinning.

"Okay, okay," I said, trying to calm them down, then thought, *fuck it*, and said, "You're all getting A's."

Millie was laughing when the class erupted once more.

Millie

It was the most beautiful thing I'd ever seen.

Stone with dark shutters, white pillars, bright-green trees, and lush, red bushes. Graceland Mansion was everything I'd imaged, and more. And that was just the outside.

It had taken us longer to get here than we'd initially thought. Trying to plan around Jackson's school schedule, and dealing with the rapid growth of Three Sisters Catering when we added elegant children's parties and landed one of our biggest clients to date, had made it difficult.

But now, six months later, we were finally in Memphis, and I was currently trying to teach Kayla about the wonder that is Elvis.

"He's the King of Rock 'n' Roll for a reason," I was explaining as we walked to the Meditation Garden. "He still holds the record for the most Top 40 hits, he was in *thirty-one* movies, made over *one-hundred and fifty* albums and singles, and has been inducted into *five* halls of fame."

"You should totally work here," Kayla said in between licks of her hand-dipped ice cream cone from Minnie Mae's Sweets at *Elvis*

Presley's Memphis.

Jackson started laughing, and while normally I would have shot him a death glare, I was too happy to even conjure one up.

Jackson had totally outdone himself with this trip. When we'd decided to bring Kayla, he'd booked us a room at *The Guest House at Graceland*, where we were enjoying a weekend of total submersion into all things Elvis.

It was the best weekend of my life, and although I knew Kayla would rather be at Disneyland, and Jackson would probably be just about anywhere else, they were both enjoying watching me live out one of my childhood dreams.

Seriously, there was so much amazingness in this place, I could barely stand it.

It's not just a mansion . . . There's the Presley Motors Automobile Museum, Elvis: The Entertainer Career Museum, Discovery Exhibits, Elvis Presley's Memphis, The Meditation Garden, plus the tours of Graceland. It was so much more than I'd ever imagined.

After we were done perusing The Meditation Garden, we walked the grounds, nodding at other Elvis enthusiasts as we enjoyed the perfect weather. Kayla was between us, holding each of our hands as we swung her out. Her legs were a little too long, but she didn't care, she just held them up, laughed happily, and said, "Again," over and over.

Since she was nine and probably at least fifty pounds, my arm was starting to get tired, when I saw a sign for The Chapel in the Woods.

"Oh, can we go there?" I asked gleefully. We'd seen almost everything there was to see on the grounds, but we hadn't been to the chapel yet.

We started in that direction, and when we happened upon the

darling little chapel nestled in, I rushed toward in oohing and aahing. I had one hand on the railing, and was turning to say how beautiful the setting was, when I saw that both Jackson and Kayla were down on one knee, watching me expectantly.

I turned slowly, one hand on my stomach, the other at my throat, and moved until I was standing before them. My breath caught when I looked down and saw Jackson holding a gorgeous, three-stone rose-gold engagement ring in his hands.

The hand at my neck came up to cover my mouth.

"Millie." I was surprised when the first words came from Kayla, but I shifted to give her my undivided attention. She looked up at her dad, who nodded his encouragement, then back at me. "I know I was a brat at first, and I did what I could to push you away, but that's only because I was afraid to like you, then have you leave. And, even though you freak out over Elvis, and spend way too much time kissing my dad, you're pretty cool. You make all that good food, and bake me cookies when I want, and I like helping you in the kitchen. Plus, you have pretty cool sisters, and I've never had aunts. So, my dad and I would love it if you'd join our family, and let us join yours."

My eyes had filled with tears that were threatening to spill over, but before I could get down on the ground and pull Kayla in my arms, Jackson started to speak.

"To keep in our tradition of stealing from the greats, I want to start by paraphrasing Bronte . . . *Whatever our souls are made of, ours are the same* . . . Millie, *Camilla*, when I first met you, I was drawn in by your sweetness, your kind eyes, and *yes*, your beauty, and the more I got to know you, I realized that those weren't just attributes that you showed customers, or strange men begging you to host a tea party for them, but that they're innate. That's who you are, and so much more. I've never met anyone so attune to the needs of others, so willing and able to put other's before themselves. You're generous, loyal, and so perfect for me it's scary. I never imagined my first, first kiss in fifteen years would lead me here, but I'm so glad I waited. You're the pinch of salt we needed to spice up our lives, and I'm grateful that someone as amazing as you would fall for a romantic literature nerd like me. I'm hoping that sometime in the near future, we can come back here to this chapel, or meet at any chapel in the world, and you'll do me the honor of becoming my wife."

"And, becoming my mom," Kayla added.

So, I stood there, near to bursting with happiness in the most magical place on earth, and cried, "Yes, I'd love to be your wife, and it would make me happier than anything, to be your mom."

Then, *finally*, I dropped to my knees and kissed Jackson with all the love I felt for him, as Kayla hugged us both tightly, and we agreed to become the family that we all needed.

The End.

Stay tuned for Tasha and Jericho's story, A Touch of Cinnamon, coming in early 2018!

Check out the first Chapter for Bethany Lopez's, Always Room for Cupcakes:

Always Room for Cupcakes

PROLOGUE

One day you're be-bopping along, jamming to the music in your head while wondering if your thighs can handle grabbing a cupcake on the way home. The next thing you know your entire world crashes and burns.

I used to wake up at night in a sweat, crying because I'd dreamt that my husband was cheating on me, or that he hated me and resented my kids. He'd always hold me close and tell me it was all just a dream, that he loved me and our family and that he'd never let me go.

He was a fucking liar.

Instead of being the sweet, affable, hard-working man he projected to me and the outside world, he was actually a cheating, vagina-licking asshole, who only cared about getting off and being free of responsibility.

I'd gone from sweet and caring housewife to bitter, hard-as-nails single mom, who worked her ass off to give her kids a quarter of the life they were used to. Putting my photography skills to use, I'd gone to work for a scumbag PI. He used me to dig up dirt on his clients.

I was happy to do it.

I was doing a public service for women like me who thought

the men in their lives could actually be trusted, and I *really* enjoyed my job.

I'd learned quickly that men suck, my children are my saving grace, and there is *always* room for cupcakes.

ONE

"Get it in focus this time, Lila . . . none of that grainy shit you sent me last week. I need to actually see what's going down, or in this case, what's entering what."

"Ugh, thanks for that mental image, Moose," I said with a grimace into my cell. "It's bad enough I have to see that shit through my lens, I don't need you constantly talking about it."

"Quit your bitchin' and get me some good shots. This one's a high roller."

"Got it, boss," I replied, and pressed *end* on the call.

My boss may be a creepy, low-life PI, but he'd taken a chance on me when my douchebag ex left me high and dry. So even though I regularly gave him shit, he knew I'd do anything for him.

Especially if that meant a more lucrative paycheck.

That's why I was currently scrunched down in my caravan outside a seedy hotel, a half-eaten sandwich on my lap and my camera at the ready.

Moose got the clients, then hired me to get the goods. This usually involved taking pictures of men, and women, having affairs, but sometimes it was as easy as following someone and snapping a shot of them being somewhere other than where they were supposed to be.

Being a wronged woman myself, I didn't feel guilty about catching liars and cheaters in the act. I just wish I'd had an inkling that there were problems in my own marriage, and had thought to hire someone like Moose and me to get evidence against *The Douche*. Instead, I'd been clueless.

I thought my twelve-year marriage was perfect. I was a doting housewife, who'd loved raising our kids, keeping the house spic and span and having a hot meal ready for our family dinners every night. My husband made good money, we had a nice house, and we lived in a neighborhood where the kids could play outside and we didn't have to worry.

Then, one day he was supposed to be out with his buddies watching the game at a local bar, and Elena, one of our twins, had a sharp pain in her stomach that wouldn't quit. I got scared and tried to call him, but he didn't answer. Since our town was small enough that I could drive around it in fifteen minutes, I packed the kids in the car and went to the bar.

Imagine my surprise when neither he nor his buddies were there. Figuring I got the place wrong, I activated the phone finder app I'd installed on all of our phones and ended up in the parking lot behind Starbucks.

Seeing some movement in his car, I told the kids I'd be right back and jogged over to the vehicle, which, although it didn't register at the time, had foggy windows.

Filled with worry over our daughter, I didn't think, I just acted, and yanked the car door open. That's when I saw Slutty Shirley Finkle, legs spread wide, bare cunt lifted in the air, with *my* husband's face buried nose deep inside.

"You mother-fucking son of a whore!"

Yup, I'm pretty sure those were the exact words I'd yelled in the

Starbucks parking lot before snapping a picture with my phone and hightailing it out of there to take my kids to the hospital.

Now my kids and I lived in a shitty three-bedroom apartment in The Heights. I worked for Moose, and picked up shifts at my best friend Amy May's bakery whenever I could. They saw their dad most weekends, while *I* avoided him at all costs.

He'd humiliated me, broken my trust, and made me feel like an idiot for having such blind faith in him all of those years. I hated everything about him. His blond wavy hair, his chiseled jaw, and the stupid way he looked in a perfectly tailored suit. I wanted no reminder of the life we had together, except for our beautiful children, of course, which was why I'd left all of our material possessions behind with him and the house we'd once shared.

And as I watched a slick-looking middle aged man guide a heavily breasted, much younger woman into the seedy motel, I thought, *this one's for the sisterhood*. I pumped my fist as I watched them walk back out of the office and down a few doors, then got ready to strike.

First floor . . . nice.

At least this time I wouldn't have to climb anything.

When I'd first started out, about ten months ago, I'd been woefully out of shape. After being chased down the street by a heavyset woman wearing only a teddy and almost getting tackled, I'd decided it would be in my best interest to join a gym and take up running.

It made all the difference. Sometime I had to get creative, but, *knock on wood*, I always got the shot . . . even if it was sometimes grainy.

Taking pictures of people in the act is actually easier than you might think. People are stupid. Especially the ones who think they're untouchable, they'll never get caught, and that their shit don't stink.

I eased out of the van, looking around the mostly empty parking lot as I walked casually toward the door they'd entered. I even started whistling, just to make myself more conspicuous.

Hiding in plain sight actually worked.

"Thanks for leaving the curtains cracked," I murmured as I slid up to the window, camera up and ready, and peeked inside.

Unfortunately for me, but fortunately for my pocketbook, they'd left the lights blaring and must have done some heavy petting in the car, because they were already going at it.

"Sixty-nine . . . *classic.*"

I snapped quickly, making sure their faces were in frame as I captured each lick, suck, slobber, and moan.

"*Gross,*" I grumbled as I hurried back to my car.

One of the downsides of the job was that it sometimes took hours to get the sordid visions out of my head. On occasions like these, there was one thing that helped ease my pain.

I needed a cupcake.

Always Room for Cupcakes, the Cupcake Series, book 1, is Now Available on all retailers!

About the Author

Award-Winning Author Bethany Lopez began self-publishing in June 2011. She's a lover of all things romance: books, movies, music, and life, and she incorporates that into the books she writes. When she isn't reading or writing, she loves spending time with her husband and children, traveling whenever possible. Some of her favorite things are: Kristen Ashley Books, coffee in the morning, and In N Out burgers.

CONNECT WITH ME:

www.bethanylopezauthor.com

Facebook, Goodreads, Pinterest, Google +,Tumblr, Instagram

Acknowledgements

Allie at Makeready Designs. I LOVE this cover soooo much!!! Seriously, it's my favorite one yet. Thank you so much for always bringing my stories to life!

Kristina at Red Road Editing, for always making time for me. I hope you know how much I appreciate you!

KMS Freelance Editing, for helping me fine tune and get it ready for the public.

Christine Borgford of Type A Formatting, for making time for me in your busy schedule and making my pages look better than I could have hoped.

My early Alpha and Beta readers: Raine, Lori, Ann, Jennifer, Christine, Claudia and Autumn. I always appreciate your time and the feedback you give me. I can't thank you all enough!

To Jessica, from Inkslinger PR, thanks for everything. I'm so excited about the boxes you helped me put together for the Bloggers and Bookstagramers! You are Amazing!

Finally, my family. I love you guys. Thanks for always supporting me.

Made in the USA
Middletown, DE
22 November 2018